PUFFIN BOOKS

THE STOVE HAUNTING

When Danny moves to the Old Rectory in Winterstoke with his mum and dad he has the strangest feeling that the house is somehow welcoming him back . . . that he has always been there. This strange sensation is reinforced by the discovery of the old kitchen range behind a wall, and for some inexplicable reason Danny is overcome with disgust and fear. He knows his fate is inextricably linked with that dirty old stove; it harbours some secret which fills him with terror. It draws him closer and closer, at every moment it seems to haunt him, even to talk to him, until its power sweeps him back in time to a year of great unrest . . .

He is Daniel the stove-boy who is faced with a terrible choice, a test of loyalties. Should he support his friends fighting against injustice, or protect his master and his own security?

A powerful and dramatic story based on the events surrounding the prosecution of the Tolpuddle Martyrs.

Bel Mooney is a distinguished journalist who more recently has turned her talents both to broadcasting and novel writing. *The Stove Haunting* is her first novel for older children. She lives near Bath with her husband, Jonathan Dimbleby, and their two children.

THE STOVE HAUNTING

Bel Mooney

Illustrated by
Jeremy Ford

PUFFIN BOOKS

PUFFIN BOOKS

Published by the Penguin Group
Penguin Books Ltd, 27 Wrights Lane, London W8 5TZ, England
Penguin Books USA Inc., 375 Hudson Street, New York, New York 10014, USA
Penguin Books Australia Ltd, Ringwood, Victoria, Australia
Penguin Books Canada Ltd, 10 Alcorn Avenue, Toronto, Ontario, Canada M4V 3B2
Penguin Books (NZ) Ltd, 182–190 Wairau Road, Auckland 10, New Zealand

Penguin Books Ltd, Registered Offices: Harmondsworth, Middlesex, England

First published by Methuen Children's Books Limited, 1986
Published in Puffin Books 1988

Copyright © Bel Mooney, 1986
Illustrations copyright © Jeremy Ford, 1986
All rights reserved

Printed in England by Clays Ltd, St Ives plc
Set in 9 on 11½ pt Linotron Baskerville

for *Daniel Dimbleby*
who is interested in the past

CONTENTS

1 Just an old stove   9

2 Into the blackness   18

3 Friend George   28

4 A child's cry   38

5 Samuel Smith   47

6 The meeting   58

7 The warning on the tree   68

8 The secret ceremony   78

9 The spy   88

10 Hunted   102

11 Tried and transported   112

12 George's promise   126

13 In the churchyard   141

Chapter 1

JUST AN OLD STOVE

'The trouble with these old houses is that they need so much doing to them,' said Daniel's mother, as she scratched at the banister with a sharp paint scraper, making curls of old paint fall to the floor. Daniel screwed up his face because the stuff she was using to remove it had such an awful smell.

'Well, why don't you just leave things as they are?' he asked, kicking at the uncarpeted stairs, so that the clunking noise echoed through the old house.

Eve Richards sighed. 'I can promise you that you wouldn't like that at all, Dan! If this house had been left untouched for years it would be a mess: no bathrooms, no heating – you wouldn't enjoy that, would you?'

'But I don't enjoy this either,' Daniel said, looking around.

They had moved in just two days before. The huge furniture van had trundled all their possessions from the neat terraced house in South London – which Daniel loved – to this rambling country rectory, which he felt unsure about. He remembered that dreadful moment during Sunday lunch when his parents had looked across the table at each other in a serious and secret way. His father had said, 'Dan, we've something important to tell you.'

'Darling, you know Dad and I have always wanted to leave London and move to the country?' his mother said brightly.

'Well,' his father went on, almost as if they had rehearsed this speech, 'I've managed to find a partnership in a small group practice in Somerset. We went down a few weekends ago, when you were staying with Bernard. It's a smallish surgery which serves several villages, and we've found a wonderful old rectory in one of the villages. It's called Winterstoke. It's really pretty, you'll like it.'

'Like a picture postcard, I suppose,' said Daniel sourly. But they did not hear.

Daniel's mother's eyes shone and she clasped her hands. 'Oh, I'm so excited, Peter,' she said to Daniel's father, quite forgetting about her son. 'Just what we've always wanted, and at last! I'll be so peaceful, and I can make that light room at the top into a sort of studio and set up my work table. I think I'll look out for a second-hand loom and teach myself weaving . . .'

She rattled on. They both did – leaving Daniel out of

their conversation. He sat, thinking of the alien country-side, the hum of London traffic gone for ever, and all the new people to meet. It was not fair, he thought, that adults always made their plans without asking children.

A day or two later Daniel made his complaint to his father as he sat wearily in the armchair after evening surgery. Dr Richards smiled as he opened the newspaper.

'Of course we don't ask permission, Dan, because children don't necessarily know what's best.'

'But how do you *know* we don't?' Daniel protested.

His father put down the paper and looked at him with a gentle twinkle in his eye.

'Because, Danny, I'm forty and you're just eleven, which means I've lived for twenty-nine years longer than you have. So I tend to think that grown-ups know best, and that they always have.'

Daniel frowned. 'But Dad, what about the fact that grown-ups have often got things wrong? All through time! I don't think anyone *knows* what's best, they just *think* they do.'

Dr Richards shrugged. 'It's quite a good argument. But look, I'm talking about this one family. All I say is that once you've got used to village life, I know you'll love it. There's a good small school you can walk to until the end of this year. Then there's a daily bus to Newtonstowe School and you'll go with the other village children. It's healthy and it's safe. Wait and see.'

So, seven weeks later the Richards family moved into the Old Rectory in Winterstoke. The village was not as small as Daniel had imagined. There was a square village green, with a huge thick oak tree in the middle, and cottages all around. At one end of the village was the church with its square Norman tower, and the splendid manor house in the distance. A new rectory – a plain modern bungalow – had been built at the bottom of the hill, near the church, and the Old Rectory looked down on them both. It was a handsome stone house, with five bedrooms and a huge rambling garden, put to grass and shrubs. A tall stone wall ran all round this garden, giving it an air of peaceful secrecy. Rooks cawed in the cedars in the churchyard down the hill. All around stretched the rich farming land, green and brown, and still divided by ancient hedgerows, full, in the pale spring light, of ragged pink, yellow and mauve flowers, which Daniel could not name.

Facing the village green was the old school, with the date 1860 carved in stone on its gable. It had been turned into a small village hall, whilst a new school – a pleasant, long, low building which combined old and new styles of architecture – stood at the opposite end of the village, near a cluster of newish houses, all with pale green front doors. The rest of the houses were cottages built in mellow greyish-gold stone, many of which had had extensions added, often spoiling the shape of the house. Winterstoke had one shop which sold everything, and a tiny pub called 'The King's Head'. Eve Richards kept saying what a perfect place the village was, but Daniel longed for the pavements, brightly-lit shops and dull growl of London buses.

The house was in chaos. Packing cases stood everywhere, spilling their contents on to shelves and window-sills. But friendly neighbours called, and soon women with kind faces were busy helping the new doctor and his wife. The way they spoke, the odd sound they gave some words, fascinated Daniel. Although he would not admit it to his parents, for he did not want to appear to give in so easily, he secretly liked their new house, with its curious jutting gables, the ornately carved mouldings round doors and windowsills, and the pointed front door.

'Victorian Gothic,' his mother said knowledgeably. 'That door must have been added in the mid-nineteenth century when there was a craze for the style. The house is much older: I believe it was a farmhouse in the eighteenth century, and then became the rectory.'

'Those old rectors had plenty of money then?' Daniel asked.

'Oh, yes! Much more than now. No vicar could afford to heat this now,' smiled his mother, staring around the spacious hall with its huge leaded window.

From the outside, the Old Rectory looked like the kind of building you sometimes see illustrated in ghost stories: tall and ivy-covered, with a look of mystery about it. Yet the house was not at all spooky inside. It had a friendly feel to it, as if it welcomed the new arrivals. It had stopped being a rectory twenty years ago, Eve Richards explained to Daniel, like so many rectories – quite simply because of money. 'Some have been turned into small hotels and some into private houses, like this one. And some have just become derelict, I suppose,' she said.

'That would be sad,' said Daniel.

After the first excitement of arrival had worn off, and Daniel had made his bedroom as much like his old one as possible, he began to feel resentful. It was the builders: in no time at all there was a van outside the house and pots of paint in the hall. Somehow he had imagined that they would simply move in, hang pictures, and get on with life. But no, Mrs Richards had decided they needed extra central heating, a new bathroom, more bookshelves, a good deal of new wallpaper and paint, and – worst of all – a new kitchen. She had chosen smart pine kitchen units from a glossy brochure to replace the ugly pale blue ones someone had put into the house in the fifties or sixties.

'I wouldn't mind if it had been left as a splendid traditional country kitchen,' she sighed. 'But one of the odd things about moving into really old houses is that you have to try to put it back as it once might have been.'

'That's just stupid,' said Daniel, who hated all the fuss.

So the builders arrived early to start ripping the kitchen apart and Eve Richards scraped away at her banister, because she had decided it would look better in polished wood than painted white.

Feeling bored and useless, Daniel wandered into the kitchen to watch the men. The older one of the two, a big man called Harry, was sitting at the kitchen table drinking tea from a steaming flask. The younger man, Bill, was standing with his hands on his hips, staring at the blank wall at the end of the kitchen.

'That's where it must have been, Harry,' he was saying. 'You can still see the mark where the mantlepiece must have been.'

Harry made a slurping noise with his tea and nodded. 'These old places have been pulled about right enough. Makes it hard to know what we're doing,' he grumbled.

They nodded at Daniel, who asked what they were doing.

'Just working out the new plumbing, my lad,' said Harry. 'And these walls, some of them, they're thick as a tree.' They went on mumbling about 'runs' and 'cavity walls' and clumped about on the tiled floor with their heavy boots.

Bored, Daniel turned away and went into the garden. He stood gazing at the crisp green of the distant fields, contrasting with the bright yellow of the daffodils, which dotted the lawn and nodded in clumps under the beech trees. There was a feeling of movement, of growth, in the air – as if he might strain his ears and even hear the shoots pushing upwards through the soil.

'You never feel that in London,' he thought, 'except sometimes in the parks. It's not like this, it doesn't . . . take you over, somehow.' Again he had the oddest feeling, that he had always been in this place; that it was welcoming him back.

It was a long time later, after he had explored the garden for the hundredth time, considered making a vegetable plot of his own, and daydreamed about a tennis court, that he heard the shout from the kitchen. The dull crashing thuds of the sledgehammers had stopped.

'Mrs Richards!' called Harry's voice. 'Come and look at this!'

Full of curiosity Daniel turned towards the house. Something was happening at last. As he pushed open the back door, which led in turn to the kitchen, he could smell the dust. It filled his nostrils with its dead, choking scent, seeping through the closed kitchen door like steam and

15

making him catch his breath. Then, when he opened the door itself, he gasped. Dust hung in the air, almost obscuring the figures of his mother and the two builders. They were standing and staring at something in the wall beside him, and Bill was saying with satisfaction, 'There, an' I thought 'e'd be there.'

'What are you looking at?' asked Daniel, coughing slightly and screwing up his eyes against the cloud of fine dust. 'What a horrible smell!'

'Look, Dan, look what they've found,' said Eve, pointing. Buried treasure was the thought in his mind, as he moved across the room to join them; or perhaps a skeleton hidden away in a secret cupboard in the wall.

But it was nothing like that. As he looked in the same direction, Daniel felt a curious sensation that was a mixture of disappointment and (this he could not understand) disgust. 'Why, it's just an old stove,' he said.

There, visible through a huge gaping hole in the plasterwork of the wall, was an old kitchen range. It was massive and black, though streaked with rust and covered with dirt and cobwebs. As Daniel stared, a piece of brick suddenly dislodged itself and fell down on to its surface, so that they all jumped, and an enormous spider scuttled across from one corner of the range to the other.

'Ugh!' said Eve with a shudder. 'It's a ghastly old thing.'

'That's what they used to cook on, Missus,' said Harry cheerfully, adding with a laugh, 'back in the good old days.'

'Bad old days, you mean,' said Eve, smiling at Daniel. 'What do you think of that relic, eh, Danny?'

'Yuk, it's horrible,' he said, staring at the thing. 'How could they ever have cooked on it?'

'Lord knows,' she shrugged.

Daniel could not take his eyes from the old stove. It seemed to fill the room with a peculiar smell – of dirt, dust, damp and the decay of years. It was a clinging unpleasant aroma which tickled the back of his nose, and stung his throat and eyes, making him swallow hard. And as he stood, unable to move, looking at this thing the builders had found buried behind the plaster of the wall, Daniel found – to his astonishment – that he disliked it. Resentment against it made him frown suddenly, and turn sharply away, with his hands thrust sullenly into his pockets.

But there was more to it than that. With no explanation, Daniel's heart started to beat just a little faster as he left the room, and he knew it was fear that he felt – fear at the sight of the stove.

He did not *want* it to be found.

Chapter 2

INTO THE BLACKNESS

'It's quite a find,' Dr Richards said when he came home that evening. The builders had swept up most of the dirt and Mrs Richards had finished with the vacuum cleaner, and now the three of them sat in the middle of the kitchen staring at the old stove. They ate ham sandwiches and drank soup from mugs.

'Oh, I don't like it at all,' Daniel's mother said. 'Imagine having to slave over that all day, cooking huge meals for the vicar's family.'

'*You* wouldn't have had to,' said Daniel.

'What do you mean? Of course I would!'

'No, you'd have been the lady of the house. Everybody had cooks in the olden days; we did it in history,' Daniel replied, taking a large bite and chewing it with satis-faction.

'The cooks didn't have cooks,' Dr Richards said quietly.

'No,' said Daniel. 'It was the cooks what slaved.'

'*Who* slaved, dear,' murmured his mother.

Daniel rose and wandered over to the old kitchen range. Now that the builders had stripped away all the plaster it was easy to see where the stone over-mantle had once been, and there was even a chunk of iron left in the brickwork, where there had once been a hook or bar to hang things from. The stove sat squarely in the middle of its hole in the wall, as if the house had been built around it. There was a kind of grating with bars in front of it, behind which the fire used to be lit, with a handle sticking out.

'What was this for, do you think?' asked Daniel, pushing it up and down with a harsh, clattering sound.

'Well, I suppose it might be something to do with the way they controlled the heat. I suppose if you moved it up you'd raise the firebase and the hot plates would get hotter.' Daniel's father had risen too, and stood next to his son, gazing at the blackened hunk of iron in their kitchen wall.

'Look, Dad, it says something here!' said Daniel excitedly, brushing with his fingers at a metal plate on the front of the stove. Dr Richards bent down.

'Let's see . . . the . . . er . . . *Herald Patent*. That's the name of the maker. Mmm, it's really interesting.'

Mrs Richards was still sitting at the table, leafing through her pile of kitchen brochures.

'The point is this, you two history maniacs,' she said

impatiently, 'what are we going to do about the thing? It's taking up an awful lot of valuable space. I was going to put pine cupboards along that wall.'

Dr Richards frowned. 'I know what you're saying, Evie, but it's, well . . . it's a sort of monument, isn't it?'

'I don't particularly want monuments in my kitchen, thank you very much. It's not a museum, it's a home. It'll have to come out.'

'Mum!' shouted Daniel, suddenly realizing what she was saying. 'You can't just rip it out. We can't just find it, and then . . .'

Then, to his own surprise, Daniel fell silent. He wanted to explain how you should try to preserve things, because that was something they had talked about at school, but no words would come. For a second it was as if his parents were suddenly very far away from him, small faces and tiny voices in the distance, whilst he stared at the *Herald*, and could think of nothing else. Black and dark and full of mystery it looked, and yet he *knew* it, somehow, as you know – well, your own hand. He held up his hand and stared down at his palm.

'*Black* . . .' he whispered.

'What did you say, darling?' asked Eve Richards.

Daniel looked up, a puzzled expression on his face. 'What? Oh, I don't know, what did I say?' He dropped his hand to his side, feeling puzzled and silly.

'Are your hands dirty?' asked his father.

'No . . . er, no,' Daniel replied, staring at the stove, hardly hearing.

'Well, I'm going to put my feet up and read the newspaper,' said Eve Richards, 'and then I'll have to sort out the clothes. Honestly, I'm never moving house again!'

'I'll help you,' said Dr Richards.

'Don't bother about me, I'll just stay here for a bit,' said Daniel to no one in particular. He needed them to go out, to leave him, for he found himself wanting to touch the stove in a way that would be totally private, and which he did not understand.

When he was alone in the kitchen, he sighed and looked at the stove again. Something drew him to it – and yet, he thought, that was not really so surprising. He liked old things, and history was his best subject at school. *School!* The thought reminded him that on Monday he would have to start at the village school, and meet strange boys and girls who might laugh at his unfamiliar accent. He would feel *different*. He shivered at the prospect.

'But I am different,' he said aloud in the silent room, and then jerked his head in surprise. Why had he said that? He knew in his heart that he had not simply been talking about his voice, his accent, and how it would stand out in this new part of the country; nothing so simple. Something else, something inside him was different. He knew it.

He remembered the night, shortly before they had moved, when he had crept downstairs, and heard his parents talking in the sitting-room.

'I just worry about him, that's all,' his mother had said, and Daniel had known right away she was discussing him.

'Oh, he'll be all right,' his father had replied. 'He's just a bit of a loner, that's all. He dreams a lot. I used to be like that.'

'Yes, but I wish he had more friends,' Mrs Richards said sounding anxious again. 'If only . . .' In that second her voice changed and she suddenly sounded terribly sad.

Daniel heard his father get up. He must have gone over to her chair. 'I know what you were going to say, my love,' he murmured in a gentle voice. 'If only our baby hadn't died. But we can't change things, can we?'

'Daniel would have had a little brother, then he wouldn't be so lonely,' she sighed.

'Now, Evie, he's not lonely, he's just sensitive and likes being on his own. Maybe he's a bit timid and needs to build up his confidence a little, but that's very different.' Dr Richards's voice was brisker now. 'He's just fine, and I bet you he'll settle down really well in Winterstoke. It's just the place for a boy like Dan. Country children . . . well, they're gentler than city kids, I always think. He'll find his feet with them.'

'I hope you're right, Peter, but . . . oh, I expect you are,' she said.

Then it had sounded as if they were getting up and so Daniel had scuttled quickly up the stairs and jumped into bed. 'We can't change things,' his father had said, and those words echoed strangely in his mind. Not that there was anything he wanted to change very much, although he would have liked a brother, and, more importantly, would have liked his mother not to be sad. But how could you alter what had happened? It was impossible, and so you just went on putting up with it all, he supposed. *We can't change things*.

He looked up quickly. It was as if those words came from outside him, not simply from inside his memory. Yet the idea in the words was a part of him too, far beyond memory itself, more a part of his blood and bones. And something was making the words be said, there in the kitchen, dominated by the old cast iron stove which had fed the people who had lived in this house for years and years. Hands must have stirred and poked and cleaned and shovelled, hands must have grown black with dirt from the stove.

'Black,' said Daniel aloud, looking at his hands again with a frown. But his own hands were surprisingly clean. There was no soot on them, no grease from the stove, and yet – this was the feeling that astonished him – he sensed that there *should* be. 'Black? Where is the black?' he whispered, searching deep in his mind for the answer to . . . but what? He blinked and shook his head.

He reached out one finger towards the *Herald Patent* and slowly traced a line in the faint powdering of dust that still lay on its surface. He spread out his fingers and stroked the old metal, as if in a dream. Then suddenly he drew back his hand sharply, as if he had had an electric shock. How could it be? Reaching out with just one finger, he touched the top of the stove again, to make sure. It was impossible, but yes, it was slightly warm to his touch. The cold black iron, which had lain undiscovered for he did not know how long, was warm as though the fire had only gone out the day before.

Daniel ran from the room and across the shadowy hall into the sitting-room.

'Dad! Dad! Can you come here for a moment?' he called, trying to make his voice sound normal.

His father groaned and heaved himself to his feet. 'Oh,

Dan, what is it now? Can't I sit down for five minutes?'

'Just come into the kitchen with me, Dad. I'm doing . . . er . . . an experiment!'

They reached the stove. 'Well, what is it?' asked Dr Richards, still with impatience in his voice.

'Can you just hold your hand against the top?' asked Daniel nervously. His father did as he was asked, then looked at Daniel with a puzzled face.

'Well, what now?'

'How does it feel?'

'Like a lump of old stove! What do you think it feels like?'

'Is it . . . is it warm, Dad?' Daniel blurted, feeling his face redden.

Without saying anything, Dr Richards seized Daniel's own hand and placed it, palm flat down, on one of the old hotplates. It was icy cold to his touch. Daniel shivered.

'I don't know what scientific experiments you're trying to conduct, Sonny Jim, but I'm going back to my armchair,' laughed his father, and left Daniel alone in the kitchen once more.

It was nearly dark now. A great quietness seemed to have fallen on the room, and it seemed as though the house – containing his parents, all their furniture, the books in their boxes waiting to be unpacked, and the pictures not yet hung on the walls – had melted away. When Daniel looked at the stove his toes tingled and his eyes prickled, as if he were about to cry. Yet he had no idea why he should cry, or for whom.

Once again, he reached out; then pulled back his hand, dreading to find that the stove really did feel warm. *We can't change things*. This time he definitely heard those words outside himself, like a whisper in the room, as gentle and resigned as the fall of leaves in autumn, drifting to the ground.

'But what can't we change?' he asked aloud. 'It can't mean the future, because we can change that all right. But the past – we can't change the past.'

The house seemed to return to normal in an instant. The sound of the television was reassuring, and his mother was singing in the hall as she unpacked a box with a clattering noise.

'I wonder what this thing is like inside,' Daniel muttered, and tried to open one of the oven doors. It was stuck: the metal bar which secured it would not move. So Daniel went to the sink, picked up a knife, and started to take its sharp edge very carefully along all the joints and cracks of the stove. Slivers of caked rust and dirt fell to the floor, and – strangely – Daniel seemed to hear them falling, like a miniature rockfall.

'Should . . . come . . . now,' he grunted, putting both hands on the latch and heaving it up. Still nothing happened, but he felt an odd tremor run through his body, as though he himself were being pulled by a giant force, pulled slowly up and up, like the stout metal bar. There was a harsh grating sound as metal moved on metal. Daniel dropped to his knees and pushed with all his strength until the latch gave way. As it did so, a wave of dizziness swept over him, so that he had to support himself with one hand on the top of the stove. It was warm – as it had been before! The hairs on the back of his neck stood up and he started to shiver uncontrollably.

Daniel had always believed in hauntings. When he had first seen their new home he had wondered, for he borrowed collections of ghost-stories from the library and had a vivid imagination. But all the bustle and activity of moving had banished the suspicion, and the noise of hammers and drills gave no space for quiet imaginings. Now it returned. He noticed, with a feeling of sick dread and shock that he had never before experienced, that the house had grown completely silent now: no television, no singing; all had faded away as if they had never been. And now his hands were pulling open the old oven door. With an unpleasant, wheezing sound it released itself, so that Daniel could peer inside. There was one slatted iron shelf, and the oven walls were dappled with red rust on black. He found himself tutting with disapproval, as if somehow it was his fault – as if he had failed in a duty. But what duty? He shook his head to rid himself of the awful feeling of guilt that had descended on him. Something had happened. He knew it. There was nothing he could have done, for *we can't change things*. No, we can't.

He was on his hands and knees in front of the *Herald Patent* staring into the black mouth of one of its ovens, and hearing those helpless words coming, it seemed, from inside the dark opening itself.

'Who is it?' he whispered fearfully, and waited for a reply. But there was none. Only a whirring sensation in his head and a sighing sound in his ears, as if from a sea-shell; but instead of the sense of wind and waves there was a falling, a dead drifting down of the dust of years. And Daniel Richards felt himself leaning forwards, looking into the mouth of the stove as if he could find in its filthy interior the answer to the question which troubled him.

'What could I have done?' he cried aloud, as if some long dead pain were forced from him. 'I couldn't go, I couldn't!' Then it seemed that he was falling forwards with the dust, tracing a path through the webs of countless spiders, moving away from himself into the blackness. It was the black of the old stove, which he now saw smeared on both the hands he held up in front of his face. And then he gave in at last to the smooth darkness that poured in through his eyes.

Chapter 3

FRIEND GEORGE

It seemed as though he was pulling himself upwards from a deep black hole, or from the bottom of the sea – swimming up painfully towards the light. But there was little light – only a faint glow from somewhere near him and a wonderful warmth, which made him sleepy again. A voice was calling in his ear, a voice which was rich and warm, too.

'Come on, my lad, wake up! Come on, Dan, let's see you!'

The accent was strongly Somerset, he noticed sleepily.

'Dad?' he mumbled, not raising his head.

Then another voice spoke, a woman's voice: 'Oh, 'tis a shame,' she whispered. 'There's him an orphan lad for as long as anyone round here knows, and him still calling for

28

his father.' He felt a gentle hand rest briefly on his forehead, then a rougher one shake him by the arm.

'Dan! Wake up, I'm telling you! If Mrs Brennan catches you asleep, you're in trouble!'

Daniel opened his eyes. A face was looming over him, peering from the shadowy room, but he could not make out the features. He was not afraid, though; the gruff voice was kind and the large man looking at him was oddly familiar, like a half-forgotten memory. He gave off a strong smell – a mixture of soil, grass and farmyard – which was not unpleasant, but powerful and timeless.

The hand which now cuffed Daniel playfully about the ear was rough and calloused. 'Come on, laddie, *come on!*'

Daniel opened his eyes wide. 'Who are you?' he asked. The man roared with laughter, and the sound mingled with the woman's more musical giggle.

'Hear that, Annie? He don't know friend George! He don't know where he be!' And the laughter went on as Daniel was pulled to his feet.

He found himself standing in the kitchen, yet it was not the bare, knocked-about kitchen he knew, with the square picture window looking out over the garden and fields beyond, and the ugly modern stainless steel sink his mother was about to swap for a smarter version. This room was heavy with dark green painted walls, with well-stocked, shiny brown shelves and cupboards all along them. The window seemed larger and was covered by dark brown shutters, fastened by metal bars. A strange light flickered low in the middle of the room above an enormous scrubbed pine table. And there beside him, glowing slightly in its centre, was his stove. It was set beneath a carved stone mantlepiece, and a huge black kettle sat on its surface, hissing slightly as little puffs of steam escaped from the spout.

'Where . . . where am I?' Daniel cried, turning in terror to the two people who stood beside him.

The man was tall and burly, in his middle twenties, with a good-looking, weatherbeaten face. A grubby hand-kerchief was tied around his neck, giving him a gypsy-like appearance, but he was wearing a peculiar garment, almost like a dress, which was gathered across the top and hitched in by a broad leather belt, revealing trousers underneath and stout boots. His clothing reminded Daniel of the smocks worn by pregnant women, and that thought made him want to smile.

Next to the man, looking at Daniel with a sweet but worried expression, was a young woman, who had a thin, pretty face under a white cap. No hair was visible, except one curl, which escaped on to her forehead. She wore a large creamy-white apron over a plain dress of dark, coarse material, which fell to her ankles.

'You hear that, George? He don't know where he is!' Her accent was soft and rounded, like that of the village women who had helped his mother unpack. She moved her hands together nervously. But the man called George just laughed.

'Now just you stop playing them games, Dan'l,' and he reached out to give Daniel a soft rabbit-punch in the chest. It caught him off-balance and he fell back against the stove.

'Ow! It's hot!' he exclaimed, and jumped away.

30

'Well, if it were not, then you'd be in hot water yourself, wouldn't you, my lad?'

The young woman laughed at his joke, as if it were the funniest thing she had ever heard. Daniel smiled too, confused and playing for time.

It was as if he had woken in the middle of a dream; and yet he knew – from the heat of the stove and the feeling of George's hand – that he was not asleep, and this was no dream. Yet all was altered, so that he felt puzzled and silly. It was the same place and yet it was not. He knew these people and yet he did not. He realized with more bewilderment that their names came as no shock to him. Yet why were they dressed so oddly, as if for a fancy-dress party?

Unless . . . unless they were ghosts; unless this was the stove's haunting, to call up these people from the past to torment him! The sudden fear that this might be true made him shudder, despite the heat from the kitchen range, and in spite of the friendliness on the faces before him. Ghosts . . . they must be, for all houses have their ghosts, he thought.

'The lad's sickening for something, George,' said Annie.

Daniel stared at her. 'Who . . . ?' he started to say. He meant to ask, once more, who they were, but the words came out differently, and he asked, 'Who . . . am I?' in a small voice.

'He's not sickening, he's playing games,' smiled George. 'But since you ask us, young sir, I'll tell 'ee; I do believe your name to be Daniel Richards.'

The same name. They did know him. Yet how could he

be the same Daniel Richards who had finally managed to pull open the rusty oven door? Suddenly *that* boy seemed to live in another world, or in another age. Who was *he*? He, who had moved from London to Winterstoke – the loner, the dreamer, the son of Eve and Peter Richards?

He stiffened. Parts of his brain which had been jumping around with questions, slowed down and fitted together, suggesting answers. Another *age*. The kitchen with its stoneflagged floor, the heavy black pots, the dark cupboards . . . He remembered now a picture in a history book at school – that was it! Dread made his knees go weak, so that he staggered slightly. Annie darted forward to hold his arm, with a far gentler touch than George's and then led him to a little wooden stool which stood to one side of the stove.

'Just rest a while, Dan'l. You shouldn't have gone to sleep on the cold floor, after working so hard and getting hot. I shouldn't be surprised if you haven't caught a chill, lad, and you know Mrs Brennan'll do naught for you, and then the Master and Mistress'll want to know why the shoes aren't cleaned and the coal scuttles not filled.' Her soft voice rattled on, and Daniel simply nodded – to give himself a moment to think.

But the thinking made him panic again. He felt like a tiny speck of dust, whirling through space with sickening speed, out of control. Yet he was beginning to understand, even though it was beyond understanding, for what if these were not ghosts summoned up from a time long past into his own world? What if he himself were the ghost, taken back into their age instead? If *that* was the stove's haunting, then it was more terrible than the presence of mere ghosts in fancy-dress in his mother's kitchen, for what could he do to control his own presence in the past? How might he escape it?

At that moment two things happened. There was the sound of a bell and the brisk noise of a door opening.

'George Wright! I hope you're not keeping Annie from her work. There's the Mistress's bell ringing, and her still standing there talking! Hurry now, Annie!'

The woman who had entered the kitchen was short and plump, and she barked her orders in a tone which made Annie run from the room.

'Now, Mrs Brennan,' said George in an easy and confident voice, 'I just came in to bring you a nice bunch of carrots and turnips I just pulled, and a couple of rabbits for the pot. You'll be able to make one of them tasty stews with that lot.' He smiled, and the cook tried not to respond.

'Humph,' she said, smoothing her apron over her hips.

Daniel cringed beside George, knowing instinctively that this stern woman was very ready to give cuffs and blows for little reason – and that they usually landed on him.

'Daniel!'

'Yes, Mrs Brennan?'

'What do you think you're doing sitting down and resting? There's work to be done!'

To his own astonishment, Daniel heard himself reply, with great respect in his voice, 'Well, you see, Mrs Brennan, I've gone and finished all my work.'

'You scoured the floor and the table top?'

'Yes, Ma'am.'

He immediately bowed his head in some confusion, not knowing why he had said that with such conviction. It was simply that . . . that he *knew* it was true.

'You blacked the stove and lit it again?'

'Yes, Mrs Brennan, just like you said.'

'What about the potatoes?'

'I peeled 'em fine, and they're in the pot by the sink.'

As he spoke, Daniel looked across the room to the sink. Sure enough, on the wooden draining board was a black iron pot with a tall handle – and he knew that the potatoes were inside.

The cook grunted, 'Humph, well, all right then,' and seized the pot with her muscular arm, carrying it across to the stove.

'The boy were so tired with all his hard work he fell asleep on the floor,' said George in a teasing voice, which told Daniel that he was not afraid of this woman, whose frown seemed to be fixed permanently between her eyebrows.

'Sleeping!' she exclaimed. 'And him a charity child, an orphan taken in by the Reverend in his mercy! What's he got to do with sleeping? That's ungrateful, I'd say, George Wright!'

George winked at Daniel, who looked down. For the first time he noticed that he too was dressed in a smock-like garment, similar to that worn by George, and that his feet were bare. A very worn pair of odd, high-laced boots stood near the stove, and he knew by instinct that they were his. In that moment he felt more at ease in this place, with these people. It was as if the two Daniels (for he was sure there must be two) had grown together, and become one. Yet, who could be sure that they were not one and the same anyway? That the Daniel Richards who had heard his mother singing in the distance was not the *same* as this Daniel Richards, who was the kitchen boy at the Rectory in some past time? He opened his hands in his lap and recognized them, blackened as they were, as his own.

The room was quiet. Somewhere in the house notes of a piano rose and fell prettily.

'Miss Dorothea plays well,' said George to Mrs Brennan, whose face immediately softened.

She folded her arms comfortably: 'Yes, to be sure, and she being the sweetest girl too, as well as clever! They do say the Squire's son be looking at her warmly. She be a match for anyone, Miss Dorothea. And that reminds me, I thought to make some of that lemon pudding she do like so much . . .' And she turned away to begin cracking eggs into a basin.

George seized the moment. 'Now, you go and wash yourself, Dan, and get ready to come out with me.'

Mrs Brennan looked up sharply. 'What's this? George Wright, you've no call to be taking that boy anywhere!'

'Now, Mrs Brennan,' George said in a wheedling voice, 'don't you remember I asked you if I could take him round to my sister Mary's for a bite of supper, if he got all his work done? And you said, yes, just for special, like.'

The cook grunted, and turned back to her work. 'Mmmm, well, don't you be thinking you can always get him off, Wright! And don't you be coming round here in the morning, taking Annie's mind off her work. You've got enough to do yourself on the Master's glebe land.'

Only moments later George was closing the scullery

door behind them, and hurrying Daniel out into the chilly air. The sun was setting and the trees were bare, and yet Daniel remembered the spring . . . He shook his head, as a dog shakes off water. He was trying to remember something: his home in the old Rectory in the village of Winterstoke where he had moved with his parents in the spring of 1986. But where was his home, and where were they? Daniel's memory of the future became fuzzy and unreal, for how can you remember what has not yet happened? With a sense of sadness and longing he felt his parents pull back, back away from him, so that he was no longer sure whether he really knew them at all. The doubt made him terribly lonely, and he moved closer to the man beside him, as if for shelter and for friendship.

The rough muddy track beneath his feet was real enough; and the way that his feet, without socks, moved up and down inside the too-large boots.

'These boots, they do chaft my ankles,' he panted.

'Lucky to have boots at your age,' grunted George. 'I never had them. There's no lad works in this village with boots for his feet, except you. I'll say one thing, it's an easier life you do have, Dan, than any other boy in this village, and even though you do work all the hours of the day!'

Something in George's voice made Daniel glance up at him. In the fast fading light the young man strode beside him with a fierce, grim expression on his face, quite different to how he had looked back in the kitchen. It was as though he had worn a mask there, for the sake of the women. Now he looked serious, like a man with a purpose, with no time for jokes.

'I'm all right, George,' said Daniel comfortably, with no reason.

George stopped and looked down at him. 'That's what I'm telling you all the time, Dan. Just because you're looked after by the Reverend, who took you in off the parish, it don't mean to say that you stops thinking of those that's not all right!'

Daniel stared at him, not understanding. Yet he had a deep sense that he *should*, that this friend was simply carrying on with a conversation they had had many times.

'I'm trying to treat you like a man, Dan,' he said gruffly.

'I know that, George.'

'Do you, I wonder?' George said seriously. 'Well, you come with me tonight, and we're going somewhere before Mary's; I'm going to show you something that'll make those old boots feel really good on your feet!'

'But what . . . what are you going to show me?'

'You wait and see, Dan'l. But I promise you that it'll fair make you angry, my lad. And a bit of anger's what you need, to shake you out of your daydreaming by that stove of yours.'

Meekly, Daniel hung his head, hearing the teasing reproach in George Wright's voice. He wondered what on earth he could do to escape; yet at the same time the other part of him felt a passionate desire to see what the night would bring.

Chapter 4

A CHILD'S CRY

Winterstoke looked completely different. The church was there, square and black against the sky; the village green was there too, but they were the only two things that seemed the same to Daniel. Instead of the pale stone cottages around the Green, each with a greyish green tiled roof and some with brightly polished brass lamps outside, there were broken-down hovels. They slumped rather than stood, and in places their thatched roofs reached almost to the ground. There were enormous puddles around the cottages, and in front of one, a thin-faced woman was trying to sweep the water away from where it threatened to run in through her door.

'They're not like cottages at all,' thought Daniel. 'More like animal sheds, really.'

They walked on. There was a ploughed field where the old school should have been, and a small wood in place of the group of new houses and the new school. Screwing up his eyes in an effort to remember, he tried to picture the date on the gable of the old village school, but he could not. The future, his own time, was slipping away from him as he walked, and he recognized more and more of what he saw – as if the Daniel Richards of the past was taking over.

'Fletcher will be getting in the mangold crop, George,' he said as they passed a certain field.

'Ay, it's time; before the ground is solid,' nodded George, not slackening his pace.

Daniel was thinking quickly as they strode. No school . . . so when was this happening? Which age was he in? Memories of history lessons jumbled in his head, with the awareness that he must be clever and cunning. So he said, quite carelessly as if it didn't matter, 'George, I've been wondering lately if the Rector knows exactly when I was born. I'm right small, I think.'

'Pooh, you'm all right as you is – just right for eleven,' George replied. 'And I shouldn't be bothering your head with that; just be glad he took you in when your parents were dead on the parish!'

'But . . . er . . . I can't rightly remember what year this is, George.'

'Ha! I always knew you was as thick as a mangold yourself!' George laughed, slapping Daniel on the back. 'Why, it's the year of Our Lord eighteen hundred and thirty-five, and it's time you was a-growing up, my lad!'

They must have walked for about a mile and a half, and it had grown quite dark when George suddenly turned off the main track. The narrower path they were now on was very stony, and once or twice Daniel stumbled, but he was quickly steadied by George's brotherly arm. There was a smell of dung, smoke and rotting vegetation in the air. George stopped and held Daniel's arm with fingers that dug into his flesh.

'Listen!' he cried hoarsely.

A child was crying. The little voice rose and fell in the darkness, dying away on the light, cold wind. Then it rose again, and something about the tone pierced Daniel to his heart. He had heard babies cry before – outside supermarkets, or in shops when their parents refused them a toy or sweets – but this sound was different. There was such a note of pain, of terrible hopelessness in this child's cry, that it made Daniel shudder and feel, for some inexplicable reason, as if it were all his fault.

At the end of the path was a tiny house, this one truly like a hut. The walls seemed to be made of dirt or clay, and they gaped with holes. The thatched roof dropped down to the ground on each side like dirty hair round a poor and grubby face. There were holes in the thatch too, and the two small windows on each side of the door were stuffed with sacking. In the pale light of the moon the little building looked bleak and, cold. And all the time the desperate crying went on, coming from within.

The door opened as soon as George knocked, and a man clasped him warmly by the hand. He nodded down at Daniel and drew them both inside, leading them across to two rough wooden boxes that served for chairs on each side of the fire.

'Will you take a drop of beer, George?' the man asked.

He looked relieved when George shook his head and his hunched shoulders relaxed a little.

The cottage consisted of one small room, lit by two candles. An iron pot was hanging by a black chain over the open fire. The floor was trodden earth but two dirty sacks had been laid in front of the fire as a makeshift carpet. On a shelf in the wall by the fire stood two onions, placed as if they were precious objects. On the rough wooden table, which was the only proper furniture in the room, together with the bench which stood by it, was half a loaf of dark grainy bread and an earthenware pot with a knife stuck in it. The man pointed to these. 'So, will you take a bit o' bread and lard?' he asked. George shook his head again.

In one corner of the room, just where the tiny staircase curled up behind the fire, a woman sat on a pile of sacks on the floor. In her arms was a child of about eighteen months, and it was still crying. Neither parent seemed to notice the sound. It was as if they had grown so used to it that they did not bother to make hushing sounds, or even to rock the baby any more. The mother raised exhausted eyes to the visitors, tried to smile, but failed.

'I hope you're well, George?' she managed to whisper at last, as if it were almost too much of an effort to speak.

'How's the little 'un?' he asked instead of replying.

The mother seemed to shrink back on the sacks, and now made pathetic rocking movements with her bony arms.

'Bad, George, there's a fever now and he's been coughing as if his little chest would break in two.'

'And the others?' asked George.

41

'Not so bad, thanks be. Young William's started work now, and Rose went out stone-picking with the gang; and the twins done well with the lazin'.' She pointed proudly to the small sack of flour, made from the grains of wheat the family had managed to pick up after harvest, to make their bread with during the long winter.

'Do you go up and see 'em, lad?' said the man to Daniel, making him jump. ''Tis not often we have visitors here.' George nodded his head in the direction of the flight of stairs, so Daniel had no choice. He started to climb the narrow, twisting stairway, and to his relief George followed him up.

The stairs led straight into the single room which formed the top floor of the cottage. By the light of a single candle, Daniel could see that the room was crammed with beds. An old piece of material, like a ragged sheet, had been hung across the centre of the room in an attempt to divide it in two. On one side was a wide bed, covered with rough, woollen blankets, and with a home-made wooden cradle at its foot. On the other side was one small bed and a rough shelf-like structure against the wall, serving as another bed. These two had sacks instead of blankets, and held four children, who peered at Daniel. The oldest, a girl, lay on the hard shelf-bed, head bent over a scrap of sewing in her hand. The three boys shared the single bed: one scraped away at a stick with a sharpened stone, and the other two, twins with shocks of red hair, lay quietly, not asleep, but watching their brother and sister. None of them smiled at the visitors, although the oldest boy, William, nodded shyly at them. The girl looked sullen and beaten; all of them were terribly thin. Their arms were like

sticks poking out from the coarse smocks they wore, even in bed.

George greeted them, but expected no reply. It was as if these children could not speak. With the exposed, damp thatch above their heads, the piles of grubby sacks covering them, and their white pinched faces, Rose, William and the twins looked pitiful. Daniel wanted to turn away.

'All right?' he mumbled, and William made a dull, flat sound like 'Ah,' as if he had no choice but to agree.

'As right as can be expected,' said George sadly, behind Daniel's back.

Downstairs again George laid a sympathetic hand on the man's shoulder.

'Well, William, you've good children there.' He nodded. The baby had stopped crying now and George glanced across to where it lay peacefully in its mother's arms.

'See that, Dan? Quiet at last. You know why the child's been crying so?'

Daniel shook his head. He felt a cold draught cut keenly through the holes in the walls, so that the low fire brightened for a moment and the candles flickered. George was looking at him intently.

'Because he's sick, lad! Seven of them, sleeping up there in that room, and at night the rain comes in through the roof, and dirt and vermin fall on the baby's head. When the weather's really bad, the drain water runs into this room here! Sick, that baby, and no wonder! And, do you know what Mr Winterton said when William asked him for some milk for the baby? He said it was for to fatten up his pigs, so's he couldn't spare it. *Pigs*, Daniel!'

43

'And there's something else now, I haven't told you, George,' said William Fletcher, squatting by the fire, while his wife looked on and nodded as if she knew what he was about to say.

'Out with it then, William,' George said, with a frown.

'The Master said I'm to take a cut in my wages. He said it's because of how I tried to stop Rose from the stone-picking, since we thought as it's no place for a young girl – with all those men and their cursing and their talk. Mr Winterton, he said that his farmworkers had to do as he said with their children; he said he needed the labour. So, I had to give in and let Rose go, but it didn't do me no good, George, because now he's punishing me for crossing him!'

George ground one fist into the other. 'You see, Dan'l? Just what I was telling you! They think they can treat their men like beasts, but we're not beasts, we're human beings! And we'll prove it to them. Now then, William . . .'

The man looked timid. Even though he was older than George, it was clear that he felt in awe of the Rector's man.

'What is it, George?' he said, 'What can I do?'

'You must come to the next meeting at Samuel Smith's. You see, man, if they won't help us, we must help ourselves. And believe me, that's what we'm going to do!'

Mrs Fletcher put out a trembling hand in protest. 'We don't want no trouble, George,' she murmured, rocking the fretful child in her arms.

'Trouble!' George said in a low voice. 'And what's your life here, Susan, but a heap o' trouble? Nothing but bread and dripping to eat, and a bite of bacon once a week for your man, if he's lucky and no butcher's meat from one year to the next! The child's sick in your arms from lack of nourishment – and all because Mr Winterton, in his fine house, cares nothing for the way his labourers live. Isn't that trouble enough for you, woman?'

William Fletcher sighed, shaking his head. 'You'm a good man, George Wright, but you don't understand what a hard man the Master is! The Rector do treat you fair – and the boy here. You should be careful, George, for even he might change towards you if he heard you talking like that.'

'That's my business, William. You're right to say that Daniel and I do better than most folks, because the Reverend's a good man, but I've been telling the lad, that's no reason to forget your duty towards others!'

George looked fierce, so the man and his wife simply nodded. At that moment the baby whimpered, then burst into a fit of coughing that made Mrs Fletcher screw up her own face, as if each wracking sound tore her body in two. She started rocking again, crooning, 'There, there; easy, my darlin'; there, there, shhhhh . . .' But it was no good. The child started to cry again, and fought and twisted in its mother's arms. Daniel could see the angry red face, reminding him of the open mouth of baby birds in the nest, endlessly demanding, until the mother returns with a juicy worm. There was no such good luck here. The hunk of dry bread stood on the table, and the father stood helplessly, his arms dangling by his sides.

George stood up. 'We'll be on our way now, William. But you'll come tomorrow night?'

The man hesitated, then nodded silently and led them

to the door. 'I'll come, George. I'll come for you and Samuel.'

For a moment the two men stood, their arms out-stretched in a warm handshake. Daniel felt that he was witnessing a silent and solemn promise, for the men were totally unsmiling. Their unspoken comradeship left him out, and he stood there wishing he was older, wishing he understood. Then George fumbled underneath his smock and brought out something wrapped in a torn piece of paper. He held it out, saying gruffly, 'Here, I brought a bit o' cheese for you all.'

At that, a smile broke for the first time across Mrs Fletcher's worn face. She pulled herself to her feet with difficulty, still holding her crying bundle, and walked stiffly across the room to where they stood. With shining eyes she gazed at George, and held out one hand to him.

'Bless you, George Wright,' she said softly. 'I can cut a bit up small now and cook the morsel in a drop o' water and breadcrumbs for a bit of dinner for him. Thank you, George, for your kindness.'

As the door closed behind them and they turned to trudge back up the path, Daniel prayed that the crying would cease, for he knew now why he had never heard a sound quite like it. It was simply because the cry was one of pure *need* – and of terrible aching hunger.

Chapter 5

SAMUEL SMITH

Back to the village they hurried. It was very cold and seemed darker now that they had left the meagre light of the Fletchers' cottage.

'We'll have time for a bit o' supper with Mary, never fear, lad! Me and Samuel have got something to talk about.'

Daniel's stomach felt empty. He tried to remember having tea with his parents – soup and sandwiches, wasn't it? But the warmth of that glimmer of memory was whipped away by the chill wind which had sprung up, and the even colder certainty that it was another season, another time, another world away. That realization frightened him with its strangeness. Everything he knew in his own life was yet to come; but everything he did not

47

know in this other Daniel's life was slowly becoming clear to him. This quick, clumping walk in too-big boots, beside George, was rapidly becoming as familiar to him as walking beside his own father. This thought made him gasp, wanting to cry out to Dr Richards to reach out a magic hand and pull him forward into his own time, and protect him from whatever knowledge *this* life would bring him.

'All right, my lad?' George's hand on his shoulder reassured him. Although he could not possibly understand what was happening, or guess where it might lead him, Daniel knew that George was his friend, and he could draw strength from the man who now strode out beside him.

On the edge of the village they turned left along a lane which Daniel knew was called Blacksmith's Lane. He gasped to see The Forge: an open-fronted stone building, lit from within, with a tiny thatched cottage attached to one side. He knew it, in his own time, as an expensively enlarged house with picture-windows, and panelled front door and a Swedish car outside. Now he could hear the sound of the hammer from its dark depths, and the chink of metal.

Passing The Forge, they arrived at another cottage which Daniel knew. It was larger than the Fletchers' and its thick thatch was in good repair. George did not even bother to knock; he walked in as if he had a right to be there. The room they entered had a very different atmosphere from the one they had just visited. It was larger and the dirt floor had been flattened so that wooden boards could be laid down. Clean sacks covered the central area, making a soft brown carpet. There were four chairs, a high-backed bench near the fireplace, and a wooden shelf on the wall, bearing a small collection of leather-bound books. Carved book-ends stopped them from falling off, and strings of onions and dried herbs hung from beneath the shelf as well as from the ceiling. There was a savoury smell from the black pot which hung from a chain above the fire. Two men were sitting at the table, the older one writing carefully. A plump, lively-looking woman was in the act of placing a loaf near him, and they all looked up with smiles when they heard the door close.

Mary Smith came quickly across and kissed her brother on the cheek. She bent to ruffle Daniel's hair. 'You're late, brother George,' she said, trying to frown, 'and you've been keeping this poor child from his supper too!' Then she laughed merrily and slipped her arm through her brother's, leading him across the room.

'Evening, Uncle George! Evening, Dan'l!' said the younger man at the table, whom Daniel now saw to be a boy of about fifteen or sixteen. He was heavily built, with a brown, weatherbeaten face, and a wide smile. Daniel nodded shyly at him, feeling an instinctive admiration for the older boy, who now winked broadly at him, for no reason.

'Been mangold pulling, young Joe?' asked George, tweaking the boy's ear. Joe looked down ruefully at his huge, red hands, which were engrained with dirt and criss-crossed with cuts.

'Well, I feel as if the mangolds have been a-pulling me!' he said, and they all laughed.

All this time the man at the table continued writing, and

49

it seemed that the others understood the importance of his task – so that little things, like greetings, could wait. At last the scratching ceased and he put down his quill pen with a flourish. 'George!' he said warmly, 'it's good to see you, brother – and young Dan'l too!'

When Samuel Smith stood up he seemed to fill the room, although he was not a particularly big man – smaller, in fact, than George. He looked about forty; there was grey in the black hair that curled about his forehead, and lines of worry around his mouth. When he laid a hand on Daniel's shoulder to welcome him, Daniel felt great power in that touch – as if he knew that this was a man on whom you could rely for help, and trust with any secret.

'We're late because we went down to Winterton's Long Acre to see William and Susan Fletcher,' said George.

Mary looked concerned. 'And how is the baby?' she asked, wiping her hands on her apron. 'Poor thing, poor little thing!'

'Bad – just as you'd expect,' George replied. 'And things won't get any better because their Master's said that William must take a cut in his money, on account of how he didn't want young Rose to start work as yet.'

Samuel shook his head and glanced silently at what he had been writing. At last he looked up and said gravely, 'It's getting worse, George, and it'll go on getting worse unless we can do something. Winterton don't care . . .'

'None of 'em do,' George interrupted in a tight, angry voice.

'Well, brother, after we've had a bite of sup, I'll tell you what I've been thinking . . .'

'And writing,' added Joe, with pride in his voice. He

glanced up at the row of books for a second as if to say that their presence proved that his father was an unusual man, with talents even beyond those of the most accomplished hedger, thatcher and carpenter for miles around, which he was.

As Samuel started to clear his writing equipment from the table, and Mary set about bringing plain earthenware plates from the cupboard in the wall by the fire, Joe Smith beckoned to Daniel to follow him upstairs. 'Come on, Dan'l, I want to show you something!'

Daniel dreaded to see thin children crowded into a squalid room again, but this house was different. Samuel had divided the top floor into two with a wooden partition, and it smelt clean and dry. Joe put his finger to his lips as they tiptoed into one of the rooms.

'Don't wake the little 'uns,' he whispered. Two little boys of about seven and nine were asleep in one of the beds; the other bed clearly belonged to Joe. Reaching inside it, he drew out a large, clumsy-looking knife with a wooden handle on which the initials J.S. were carved. He held it out to Daniel with a proud look on his face: 'Isn't it handsome?'

Daniel took the knife and turned it over in his hand. 'But how d'you manage to buy something like that, Joe?'

'Buy it! I couldn't *buy* 'un! No, I spent every night last week helping the blacksmith, and he let me make it in the forge.'

'That must have tired you, after working on Squire's land all day,' Daniel said with amazement.

The older boy shrugged, as if that was obvious. Then he

looked serious. 'By the way, Dan, I wanted to warn you: I heard the Squire ask the Reverend Forster if he could borrow you again.'

'Borrow me?'

'Ah, remember how he borrowed you for bird-scaring, when Harry Eades's lads were both down with the fever? Oh, you won't like that much, will you? Remember how we got caught talking?' he chuckled. Daniel frowned, then, as if a television set had been turned on, he suddenly had a clear picture in his mind. The Reverend Forster had told him that he must spend five days scaring birds off one of Squire Plumptree's newly-sown fields. He had had to walk for miles to reach the spot, right on the edge of the estate by a dark and tangled wood, which made him scared in case something should creep out from it when his back was turned. From dawn to dusk he had stayed there, beating a stick against an old pail to keep the birds away. It was cold, he remembered, with no protection from the chilly wind that cut down from the hills. Worst of all was the loneliness; no one passing, no one to talk to during those long, long days, only the wild, frustrated cries of the birds for company.

But on the third day, he had been delighted to see the face of Joe Smith appear suddenly at a hole in the hedge. 'I just dropped off the cart up the lane to see how you're getting on,' Joe had laughed, and soon they were chasing each other round, throwing clods of earth. But, as bad luck would have it, that was just the moment when Squire Plumptree appeared over the brow of the hill, riding his chestnut mare. He had broken into a gallop and arrived beside them with a face scarlet with anger.

'I only allow one boy a field, and for good reason!' he had thundered. 'Two boys is half a boy and three boys no boy at all!'

Daniel had not fully understood the meaning of this curious saying, but he understood trouble. Joe had been dispatched with a few heavy blows from the Squire's riding crop, and a couple had landed on Daniel's shoulders too, making him clench his teeth to keep tears away. When he was released to return to the Rectory, he had been summoned for a long lecture on the evils of laziness and ingratitude. But he had been lucky in one respect: the Rector did not believe in beatings.

'Oh, I hated bird-scaring!' he now hissed at Joe, 'And I hate Squire Plumptree too!' Called from below, they replaced the knife and went downstairs. Mary was pulling two nets from the pot over the fire. In one was a heap of floury potatoes, and in the other a chunk of bacon. There was butter and wheat bread on the table, and Samuel cut the bacon into chunks with his knife.

Then he said Grace: 'Father, we thank you for our food, and all thy gifts, amen.'

Daniel ate greedily, smearing butter and lard on his potatoes as he saw the others do, and breaking his little piece of bacon into slivers to make it last. But the small meal did not satisfy him. He pressed a chunk of bread into his plate to mop up the last traces of grease, and still felt hungry. Samuel, Joe and George had a small mug of ale each, and he looked at them enviously. But Mary ladled out a cupful of the hot water in which the food had been cooked: 'You'll have some tea-kettle broth?' she asked as she pushed some in front of Daniel. It tasted strange, a mixture between very thin soup and washing-up water, but Daniel finished his helping gratefully.

When the plates were cleared away, George leaned back in his chair and lit a pipe, and Samuel said, 'Well, brother George, now I can tell you what I've been doing.' He pushed the paper covered with writing across the table towards his brother-in-law.

George picked it up and began to read, screwing up his face with concentration. A smile of amazed pleasure settled on his features and he threw back his head with a gasp. 'When did you see him? How did it come to this?' he asked.

'Slowly, George, I'll tell. First I went up to the Rector after church and asked if he would see me. I waited my turn in the hall outside his study and then I came out with it, right away before he could change his mind and send me away. I told him of the hardship in the parish, George; I told him how the farmers is trying to cut the men's wages and there's children going hungry, and right on his doorstep too! I asked him if that be right, in a Christian country. So he said he would try to help; he said if I could put down all that concerns us, on paper, and give it to him to consider, he would ask Squire and Mr Winterton, and all the other farmers to have a meeting with him – and me there too, to represent the men.'

'What?' George's mouth hung open with astonishment.

'He said he'd try to get the farmers to promise not to pay any man less than ten shillings a week!'

'I don't believe it!' George let out a roar that filled the room, but Samuel held up a hand to restrain him.

'Not so fast, don't rejoice too soon, George. With the

54

good Lord's blessing it'll come to something and life may be better for the people of our village – but maybe it'll come to naught, George. The Reverend has no way of knowing whether the farmers will agree.'

As the men went on talking, and Mary Smith refilled their mugs, Daniel reached out for Samuel's piece of paper. He looked at it but could read no word on it. A part of his brain recognized the letters, but the other part could place them in no order that made sense: Daniel Richards could not read.

This realization brought with it a feeling of shocked helplessness which swept over Daniel like a wave. He was cut off for ever from everything he had been taught at school, locked into the body of this child who knew no schooling at all. Suddenly he saw knowledge, learning, as a key to freedom; at least it gave you the means to look after yourself, even though you might complain.

'So, that's decided, then?' George was saying. 'I'll get round and see William, James and Harry tomorrow – just to start with. And you'll be coming to the Rectory at six, is that right?'

Samuel nodded. But Mary looked worried and reached out to touch her husband and her brother at the same time. 'I hope . . . I hope . . . no harm comes of it all,' she murmured.

Unexpectedly, Joe broke in, 'But Mother, how can it? My father knows he has right on his side, and so how can it come to harm?'

It was obviously an unusually long speech for the boy, because he blushed crimson at the sound of his own voice. George patted him, and Samuel said gently to his wife, 'We must do what we can, Mary, harm or no harm.'

'I know,' she replied. 'But sometimes, Samuel, I do fear that things will go wrong and the powerful men will take a powerful revenge.'

As she spoke, Daniel felt dizzy. He was overwhelmed by a feeling of dread at Mary Smith's words, as if he knew something that she did not; that he should warn them. Yet what could he do, even if he could explain this sensation? For all this had already happened – everything he was witnessing had passed, years and years ago. Since that was so, what could he do to change it? Nothing. The words 'forgive me' echoed strangely in his head.

Much later, George fumbled for the hidden latch key in the blackness outside the scullery door, and said good-night – leaving Daniel to find his way alone into the dark kitchen. As he closed the door, Daniel hesitated. He was not afraid of the dark, but simply confused again; for where did he sleep? Then, acting instinctively, he went to the wooden cupboard on one side of the sink and pulled out a thin straw mattress, rolled up with a piece of old blanket. He put down his bed in front of the stove and lay down wearily.

He could not explain what had happened to him – it was a mystery far beyond his understanding. That small part of his mind which still belonged in a distant future hovered like a tiny, frightened ghost in this other world, fading rapidly as the reality of what was all around became too strong for it. And the other part of his mind, the largest part now, which *belonged* in the past, kept telling that little future phantom to stop holding on, to forget, to let it all go . . . When he obeyed, and accepted, and stopped his wondering, everything became easier. Already the first Daniel Richards was driving out all the habits, and knowledge, and memories, of the second.

The smell of that blanket, which seemed to be a part of his consciousness, gave him great comfort, and he realized why he felt so at home in this position – and why the stove the builders had discovered in the kitchen wall had reached out to him so strangely and compellingly. It was because his job was to clean it and blacken it each day; to stoke it and tend to it, and peel the vegetables that were cooked on it, and eat the left-overs from those same meals. It was because he slept at night beside it, lucky to be near its warmth when other children huddled in freezing attics. As Daniel dropped off into a deep sleep at last, it was with the knowledge that the stove was his comfort and his security, and the centre of his whole life.

Chapter 6

THE MEETING

There was no need for Daniel to ask anyone what he had to do. It seemed that the next day was taken up with a stream of orders from Mrs Brennan, so that he had no time even to think about the events of the night before.

The morning started with the cook shouting because he was still asleep when she came into the kitchen. He jumped up, put his bed away and soon found himself drawing hot water from a tap on one side of the kitchen range, and filling large china jugs for Annie to take upstairs so that the family could wash. Room by room they went, and he heard all the names of the Rector's children. 'There's Master Henry's . . . and Miss Dorothea and Miss Susannah . . . and here's for the little Masters Frederick and James . . .' Annie barely spoke to him she was so busy, and clouds of steam swirled about the stove as Mrs Brennan cooked eggs and made porridge for the family breakfast. A delicious smell filled the kitchen as she fried kidneys and bacon, making Daniel's mouth water. For a second he thought back to Fletcher's bleak hovel, and the cry of their child.

There were three doors into the kitchen. One led through the scullery into the garden – that was the back entrance to the house. The other led out into the hall with its curving mahogany staircase, and the third led into the family dining-room, divided from it by a narrow dark corridor and another door. As Mrs Brennan took the covered platters through, Daniel glimpsed the family sitting at the long table for their meal: at the head the Reverend Forster, wearing a stiff white neckcloth which emphasized his erect bearing. Daniel just had time to notice the rosy, healthy faces of the children before the door closed. He knew he could not go into the dining-room, and that although the family might be kind to him, he had to stay this side of that green baize door for ever. Theirs was the world of books and pianos, and kidneys for breakfast; his was the world of the potato peelings, the scouring brush, and black lead for the kitchen stove.

After breakfast had been cleared by Annie, and he had washed all the dirty plates in the stone sink, Daniel found a peaceful five minutes when he was alone in the kitchen. Suddenly the door opened and a boy a year or two older than himself ran into the room. It was Henry, the second child in the family and the Rector's oldest son.

'What, Dan? Not working?' he said in a friendly voice, as if he were used to teasing.

'I've finished for now, but it'll start again when she gets back,' said Daniel, smiling back at him.

Henry was carrying two odd little bats, and a shuttle-cock with real feathers, dyed a dark pinkish-red. 'There you are!' he said, handing Daniel one of the bats. He turned it over in his hand. The handle was bound in strips of red and blue leather and the tip was hollow like a drum, with a finely stretched skin each side. Daniel tapped it with his finger and it made a light rat-tat sound. The shuttlecock flew across the room and hit him on the nose.

'There! I caught you out!' shouted Henry Forster with glee. 'Come on, Richards!'

Daniel tossed the shuttlecock in the air and hit it with his bat. Henry returned it easily, but this time Daniel missed. 'That's one to me!' the other boy cried out. Daniel picked it up again, and this time they managed to keep up a rally for a few minutes, both of them laughing with delight as the shuttlecock flew higher and higher, and still each of them managed to return it.

'Now I'll get you!' Daniel shouted, drawing back his hand for a really strong hit. 'There!' And he smashed the shuttlecock with such force that it went straight past Henry's bat – and flew into the face of Mrs Brennan, who had pushed open the kitchen door at that moment.

'Oh, dear Lord!' she cried out in surprise, and just managed to avoid dropping the tray she was carrying. 'What in the name of heaven do you think you're doing, boy?' she shouted, then stopped quickly when she saw the son of the house. 'Why, Master Henry, to be sure I didn't see you.'

'It's all right, Mrs Brennan,' Henry said. 'It was my

fault. I made Richards play the game with me because Dorothea wouldn't. I'll let him get on with his work now.'

As always, when her favourite's name was mentioned, the cook's face softened. 'Oh well, Miss Dorothea doesn't want to be playing noisy boys' games, does she? You run along now, Master Henry, because Daniel has to peel all the vegetables for your dinner.'

As she turned her back to them to put down the tray, Henry Forster winked broadly at Daniel. 'Girls!' he whispered, an expression of disgust on his face. Then he went out.

As he stood at the sink later, scraping carrots in the cold water, Daniel felt a suppressed excitement – as if something very important was about to happen, although he did not know what. He heard Annie say, 'There's a lot of gentlemen coming to see the Reverend this evening, Mrs Brennan. The Squire an' all! I don't wonder that something important's happenin'.'

'If there is, it's none of your business, Annie,' snapped the cook, as she stirred something in a basin so hard that the wooden spoon rang against the china sides.

'Well, Mrs Brennan, I do think you'd be better off beating the eggs and not the bowl,' said a voice behind them, with that familiar mixture of respect and confident good humour. Annie blushed bright pink, and lowered her eyes, and Daniel realized something he had not noticed the night before – that George and Annie were in love.

George stood at the door in muddy boots, carrying a basket of eggs and a large bunch of mixed root vegetables.

'If the work's slack, may I take Annie for a turn around the kitchen garden, Mrs Brennan?' George asked.

The woman looked grudging, but Daniel could tell that, despite herself, she liked the Rector's labourer. 'Oh, very well,' she said, 'but you take Richards along with you too – I don't want any of your kissin' and nonsense.'

At that Annie threw her apron up over her face in embarrassment and ran out of the door. George and Daniel followed. The three of them set off along a narrow path, edged with bare wintry hedges, through a green door in a red brick wall, into a large open space neatly divided into rows. For a fraction of a second Daniel rolled forward once more in time, remembering that there was no such wall dividing his father's garden; it must have been pulled down years ago.

He scuffed his boots on the path, wandering off, as George stood still and took Annie's hand. He could hear his friend's words clearly on the still cold air.

'When this is all settled, I'll ask the Rector if we can wed, Annie. There's room enough in my cottage, and I'll make you a new table and two chairs with arms for beside the fire!'

'I'd like that, George,' she said simply, with her eyes down.

'It's the *future*, Annie,' George went on, almost as if he was talking to himself. 'When we get our agreement it'll all change. Working men like me will be respected, so's we can bring our sons up knowing that's their due.'

Trying not to listen, and yet listening, Daniel felt an odd sinking feeling in his stomach. It was not that he thought George was talking nonsense, because he agreed with what he said. It was just that he could not banish a suspicion that it would not happen as George thought it would, or at least not for many years.

'*There's nothing you can do to change things*,' he murmured, then jerked his head up in surprise at his own words. But George had heard.

'For shame, Daniel! That's what you was saying last week. I was telling him, Annie, that he's wrong. He may look young, but he's like an old man under that thatched head – and an old man's who's afraid!' George's tone was not jeering; he sounded affectionate but reproachful, and Daniel hung his head.

'Oh, leave the lad alone, George. I've to get back to my work,' Annie said gently.

As he walked back to the kitchen with her, Daniel looked up and asked, 'Annie, might I live with you when you marry George?'

She blushed again, and smiled. 'Poor Dan'l. You've never had a family of your own, have you, lad? Like me . . . my mother and father died when I was three.'

'So many deaths,' Daniel heard himself say, unexpectedly.

Annie looked down at him in surprise: 'Ay, lad, but it's the good Lord's will. Take George's sister, Mary, now. She lost three children after Joe, and then her old parents died, when they was put out of their cottage. But that was before you'd remember.'

'Is that why George is so angry all the time?' Daniel asked.

She looked serious. 'My George is a good man, and your best friend, my lad, and he understands things you and I know nothing of. He looks around him and he sees what's going on, and he listens to Samuel Smith and the Methodies.'

'The Methodists?' Daniel asked, with a question in his voice, which clearly surprised her.

'Why yes, Dan'l. Samuel Smith's the best lay preacher in these parts, and people do walk for miles to hear him. His master don't like it, but he can't do nothing. Samuel's the best man on his estate, and the hardest working too. There's no job that man can't do, and if he preaches his own ideas on Sundays his master accepts the bargain.'

'Is George a Methodist now, Annie?' he asked.

'Why, bless you, laddie, and I thought you knew that!' Annie said, opening the door and glancing at him as if he had gone mad. 'My George can preach a fair sermon himself when the good Lord gives him tongue.'

That afternoon, just as it was growing dark, Samuel Smith arrived at the kitchen door, his hat in his hand. He wore the smock-frock and kerchief that were George's usual dress, and yet there was something about the way he wore them which gave the simple working clothes a dignity that did not have on any other man. As he stood there, horses' hoofs could be heard from the front of the house, as the landowners arrived for the meeting.

'You could've gone to the front door, since you're expected,' Daniel said.

'No, Daniel,' said Samuel quietly, 'that would be too soon. My place is to come to the back door.'

'The Reverend said I was to take you through to the study as soon as you arrived,' said Annie, looking anxious.

Suddenly Samuel took in a sharp breath and the frown

deepened between his eyebrows. With a slight shock, Daniel realized that this man, whom the whole village admired, was nervous.

As if he could read Daniel's thoughts, Samuel said quietly, 'There'll be the Reverend Forster, Squire Plumptree, Mr Winterton, Mr Fairfax, Mr Gaskell, and maybe one or two others if the Rector could get them. It's a lot of gentlemen for one farmworker to talk to. So wish me luck, Daniel . . . Annie.' And with a nod to each, he stood by the door into the house waiting for Annie to lead him to the study.

It was nearly an hour before the door opened once more and Samuel reappeared. And a moment later, as if they understood each other by some secret sign, George Wright opened the scullery door and called out, 'Well, Samuel? Let us know what they said, man, in the name of heaven!' The other man seized George's hand and pumped it up and down. His eyes were bright.

'Our prayers have been answered, George.'

'Oh, Mr Smith!' Annie cried out, covering her mouth immediately with her hand, as if she thought she ought not to take part in this conversation. Even Mrs Brennan stood quietly, with one hand on her hip and the other clutching a wooden spoon, waiting to hear what Samuel Smith might say.

'The Masters have made a solemn promise, George,' he whispered, so quietly that the room seemed all the more silent around him, as if even the pots and pans and the old stove were depending upon the important announcement. 'I stood while they sat, George. The Reverend gave them port to drink, but I had none of it. That I don't mind; it would be strange indeed if it were otherwise. But when Mr Winterton accused his men of laziness, I was near to losing my temper.'

'Laziness!' George growled. 'An' his men working all the hours of the day and night for eight shillings a week.'

But Samuel held up his hand, and George was silenced. 'Hear me through, George, because it isn't a bad story I have to tell. The Reverend Forster was very grave all through, and explained to the Masters that there is a great hardship amongst the people of Winterstoke. He asked me to speak and I told them – all quietly like – about William Fletcher, just as one example. I told them we believe we should be paid the same as other men in other parts of the land. They asked me how much. I said ten shillings a week. At that Mr Fairfax thumped the table with his fist, and shouted that it was too much and they would never pay. But Squire Plumptree talked for a while and said that maybe they should consider a change.' He whistled. 'I couldn't believe my ears, George.'

'I wouldn't either, if I'd been there,' murmured George, shaking his head.

'In the end they said that they would pay nine shillings, George, and I agreed. It isn't what we want – not yet – but it's a good start.'

'You disappoint me, Samuel,' George said. 'We deserve the full ten shillings; the people need it to live.'

'I know, George, but we must bide our time. This is a good beginning.'

Samuel Smith's voice was firm and so George nodded. But he added suspiciously, 'How do we know they'll keep their word?'

Samuel looked triumphant. 'Because the Reverend will see they do. He took a solemn oath there and I'll never forget his words 'til I die. He stood up and said, "I stand this day as a witness between men and Masters, that the men of Winterstoke shall, if they go quietly about their work, receive for their labour nine shillings a week, and I shall undertake to see that the Masters keep their word, so help me God." ' As he recalled Reverend Forster's speech, Samuel had a look of quiet happiness on his face – almost of religious faith. Then, as if a spell was broken, George let out his breath in a long sigh, and Mrs Brennan laid down the wooden spoon on the table, and Annie let her clasped hands fall by her side.

Daniel spoke: 'So it'll be all right then, Mr Smith?'

Samuel looked down and gave him a smile of pride and relief. 'It'll be all right, Dan'l. Today sees the start of a new day for Winterstoke. Tomorrow will be better for us all, I truly believe it.'

Chapter 7

THE WARNING ON THE TREE

It was four days later. All the scenes that Daniel knew had now faded; his whole world consisted of this house in which he was a servant, and the poor village with which he felt so involved. Gradually he had come to realize the deep cause of his old argument with George. George wanted change and was prepared to take great risks to get it, but he, Daniel, was afraid. He felt in awe of the Rector to whom he owed a way of life that was at least better than that endured by the children of the farmworkers, in their chilly cottages, with no food in their stomachs. Most of all he was afraid, in a trembling way he could not explain, of the farmers, the landowners, the Squire – all those who owned the beautiful wild countryside, the rolling fields between tall hedges, which stretched for miles around the village.

'No stomach for a fight,' George teased. And that was just about right.

In church on Sunday Daniel sat at the back and saw the Squire and his family walk along the aisle to their pew just beneath the pulpit. The ladies from the Manor wore silk dresses which rustled along the stone floor, and velvet cloaks trimmed with soft fur. Mrs Forster was more quietly dressed in dark blue, with no fur, and her face was pale and serious under her dark silk bonnet as she led her five children to their own pew, and knelt down to pray. But Henry's eyes darted around mischievously and Dorothea Forster blushed under her pink bonnet. Everyone seemed to have their proper place: the gentry at the front and the labourers at the back, whilst the Reverend Forster climbed up into the pulpit and preached a sermon about loving your neighbour as yourself. 'Thus you will mirror the greater love of the Lord,' he boomed.

Daniel looked around the little stone church with its coloured glass, polished wooden pews and carved stone ivy leaves around the base of the pulpit – and he wondered. What did all this mean? Did God love those who were not here as well? Somewhere George was tramping seven miles with Samuel Smith to preach at an open-air Methodist meeting in the tiny village of Tunneford. He did not believe God lived in buildings, he said, but in the fields and in the cottages with the poor. That made Daniel afraid too. Always he worried that something might happen to his George, who was father and brother to him as well as friend, and whose kind but hot-headed moods he had come to know and love. 'Sometimes the masters do send their men to break up the Methodist meetings,' George had explained the day before. 'But what's a few kicks and blows if a man believes what he believes with all his heart? It's nothing, is it, Daniel?'

Now it was Tuesday morning, and Daniel was startled in the middle of scrubbing the table by the bang of the scullery door. It was George, with a face that was set and angry – but despairing as well.

'Where's the cook?' he demanded without even saying hallo.

'Gone to the dairy,' replied Daniel.

'And Annie?'

'Upstairs cleaning the bedrooms,' said Daniel, 'But what's . . .'

'Then draw me a sup of ale, lad. I need it.'

'Oh, George, I daren't. Not without asking Mrs Brennan,' began Daniel, but stopped when he saw George's frown. He rushed out to the pantry, fearful that he would be seen even though there was no one around, and came back with the drink. 'Oh, George,' he said as he handed it over and George took a great gulp, 'what's the matter with you? What's happened?'

'They've betrayed us, that's what's happened,' said George with his teeth clenched. 'The Masters – they went to the Magistrate to ask if they could be made by law to pay our nine shillings. And you know who the magistrate is, don't you?' His voice was harsh and scornful. Daniel shook his head. 'It's Squire Plumptree's brother, that's who – Frederick W. Plumptree *Esquire*!' Daniel had never heard him speak so bitterly. 'And of course, Frederick W.

Plumptree *Esquire* said that there is no law in this land which compels the farmers to pay their men a fixed sum.'

'But the Reverend, he said he'd see they stood by their word?'

'Ay, that he did, if Samuel is to be believed,' George nodded.

'I'd believe Samuel any day,' said Daniel.

'To be sure you would, so would any man hereabouts. Well, our Master denies he made the vow that Samuel said he made.' George banged his tankard on the table.

Daniel was horrified. 'But how can he? I thought . . . Oh George, the Reverend is a good man!'

'That's what I thought, too. But he's gone against his word because the Masters have been talking to him. The gentry sticks together, lad. They always have and they always will. And now the farmers are saying that they'll drop our wages to seven shillings, and it'll go down to six unless we keep our mouths shut and get on with the work.'

At that moment Annie came in, carrying a heavy bucket of dirty water, and George jumped up to help her. He told her the story quickly, and she began to cry quietly into her apron. 'What'll happen now, George?' she sobbed.

He took her arm and lowered his voice, speaking quickly. 'We had a meeting under the tree on the village green early this morning, before first light. Pretty near every man in the district came along, Annie. They feel betrayed, see. They always trusted the magistrates and the parsons, and now they see they can't.'

'What happened?' Daniel asked, excited now, because

71

he could see that as well as being angry, George was full of some secret he longed to tell. He was right.

George raised his voice as if he no longer cared – and as if he was preaching in public. He told Annie and Daniel how the men had gathered by the light of a single lantern, and waited silently for Samuel Smith, their leader, to speak. Standing on an old box, so that he towered above them, he told them of the betrayal.

'Some of the men groaned, but some of 'em raised their fists and cried "Shame!" Then Samuel told us all what most us already knew – how he'd worked hard all his life an' taught himself to read, and by his own labours had saved to buy his collection of books in his house. He told us how he's read about men forming trade unions in the north and in other parts of England, and he told us about a man called Robert Owen who believes that all working men are equal with their masters. Oh, you should have heard him!'

George's eyes were shining now, and Annie whispered, 'Oh, the Lord do speak through Mr Smith, I'm sure of it!'

Daniel said nothing; he was thrilled by the tone of George's voice. 'Samuel stood under the old tree as the dawn began to break,' George went on, 'and he asked us to raise our hands if we agreed with making our own trade union right here in Winterstoke – a Friendly Society of Agricultural Labourers, he called it. And every man there put up his hand!'

'But what does it mean, George?' asked Daniel, aware once again of that strange sinking sensation in his stomach, as if he knew that something dreadful was about to happen. He swallowed hard to drive it away.

'It means that us men act together as one man,' said George. 'It means that we ask each other for help, and not employers, magistrates or parsons! That's how Samuel put it, and that's how I see it. There's a man who will come down and tell us how it's done, all properly like, for we must have rules and be careful who we let into our secrets! Fact is, I shouldn't rightly be telling you this now. You'd best forget it, both of you!'

'Can I come with you?' asked Daniel. 'Can I come with you to the meeting?'

George looked at him kindly, but shook his head. 'No, lad, you're too young, and in any case, you're not a farmworker yet. No doubt one day the Vicar 'ull give you my job here on the glebe land, and I'll go elsewhere, but till then you're an indoor lad.'

At those words Annie looked horrified. 'George, don't say such things! You must keep your job for ever, and then we'll be able to be married, just like you said.'

George smiled at her gently, all the strain gone from his face. 'Oh, Annie, it all depends on many things. I may not keep my job if the parson doesn't think fit. If he finds out about what we're doing, I don't think he'll be any kinder than the other masters in these parts.'

There was the sound of a bell, and Annie rushed off to answer it. Mrs Brennan came in, so there was no time for more talking. But all day Daniel thought about what George had said, always with sickness in his stomach. And when Annie came to tell him that the Rector wanted to see him in the study, his heart jumped.

'Me, Annie?'

She nodded. 'It must be something I've done wrong,' he thought fearfully.

But it wasn't. The Reverend Forster sat at his huge mahogany desk in the study, which was lined with books in glass cases. The fire burned in the grate and shone on the bright brass fender. The room seemed crowded with furniture; it was dark and warm, and somehow Daniel did not feel afraid as he approached the desk. He stood silently with his hands behind his back. The Rector did not look up from his writing at first, so Daniel studied the top of a balding head across which the hair had been combed in long wispy strands. When Reverend Forster looked up at last, he blinked at Daniel with pale, watery eyes – kind but weak.

'You wanted me, sir?'

'Ah yes, Richards. Now I'm going to ask you to perform a small service for a neighbour, for a day or two.'

'I'm sorry, sir?'

'I mean I want you to do two days' work for Mr Plumptree at the Manor. He has guests arriving and needs extra help in the kitchen, and so I said I'd spare you for a day or two, or as long as he needs you.'

'Not bird-scaring then, sir?'

'I beg your pardon?'

'Nothing, sir.'

'Very well then, you can go now. Work well, and be a credit to this house.'

It was a fine cold day. The winter sun shone on fields and trees and the hedgerows glistened with dampness. A cart rumbled past Daniel, swaying from side to side in the uneven ruts of the muddy track, and a man waved. Even

74

the tumbledown cottages with their ragged thatched roofs looked better in the golden light, and for a few moments Daniel felt almost happy.

'I shall see inside the Manor House at last,' he whispered to himself, excited at the prospect – for the Squire and his family were important people to whom you bowed your head or touched your cap at a distance. The thought of being under the same roof as these well-dressed people, even if only for a couple of nights, made Daniel puff out his chest.

He was about to walk past the village green, with the spreading oak tree in the middle, when he remembered what had happened there, and his happiness faded a little. He hadn't said goodbye to George; there had been no time, but Annie had promised to tell him that Daniel would only be away for a day or two. Still, Daniel felt a wrench inside him; he wished he could have seen George again that day, to tell him . . . but what? 'Oh, be careful, just be *careful*, that's all,' Daniel said aloud, stopping and staring across at the old oak. He blinked in the sunlight and screwed up his eyes. Sure enough, he could see something white against the tree's bark, something like a piece of paper. He wasted no time, but trotted off over damp grass to see what it was. A large poster was nailed to the rough bark of the tree, known for miles around as the Winterstoke Oak and famous for its great age and beauty. The nails had been driven deeply into its bark. Daniel stared up at the poster, but the words which covered it were meaningless signs to him. Yet he sensed their importance; he knew that he had to find out what they said. He must find someone who could read . . . but then most of the people in Winterstoke could neither read nor write and so would be in the same position as he was. Tears of frustration filled his eyes, and he was about to turn away from the poster when he felt a firm hand on his shoulder.

'Ay, lad, this is it.'

Swinging round he saw Samuel Smith standing behind him, reading the poster with a deep frown on his brow, and his mouth set into an unusually hard line.

'What does it mean, Mr Smith?' he asked. 'What does it say?'

Samuel Smith hitched up his smock in the wide leather belt, then folded his arms across his broad chest. Almost as if he were alone he read the notice aloud, in a dead flat voice:

CAUTION: It has been made known to us from many quarters that persons with an intention of causing trouble have for some time been endeavouring to induce labourers in many parishes in this country to attend meetings, and enter into illegal societies or unions, to which they bind themselves by unlawful oaths. Accordingly, we, the undersigned Justices, think it our duty to give this public notice and caution that all persons may know the danger they incur by entering such societies . . .

Daniel looked up at Samuel with wide, frightened eyes, and cried out, 'Danger, Mr Smith? What danger?'

But the man carried on reading as if he had not noticed the interruption.

We hereby declare that any person who joins such a society, any person who persuades another to join such a society, any person who administers a solemn oath to another, or any person who takes such an oath . . .

He stopped.

'Please go on, Mr Smith,' said Daniel.

. . . shall become guilty of felony and be liable to be transported for seven years.

He looked down at Daniel, who was puzzling over the long words, and said with a grim look on his face. 'There's more writing up there, lad, but it only says the same thing in different ways. And there's names on the bottom too, and one of them is Frederick Plumptree.'

'Squire's brother?'

'The very same.'

Daniel stared as Samuel tore the notice from the tree, folded it and tucked it up under his smock.

'I'm taking this home to study,' he said.

'But Mr Smith, I don't understand,' Daniel said help-lessly. 'Can't you tell me what it all means?'

The big man reached out and laid a hand on his head. 'No doubt George 'ull explain it more to you when we've talked it through, lad,' he said kindly, the grim note disappearing from his voice for a minute. 'But I can tell you quickly. It means the masters will try to stop us men getting together to make our lot better in this parish. It's just a straight *warning* to us, lad. That's what it means!'

Chapter 8

THE SECRET CEREMONY

Winterstoke Manor was an imposing building with tall windows, a pillared front door, and warm honey-coloured stone walls. Daniel was not sure how to approach it. After all, he could hardly go up to the front door, and he did not know how to reach the back door. He felt ragged and small – sure someone would stop him.

Sure enough, as he walked round the side of the house, he heard a harsh voice shout, 'You, boy! What are you doing?' He stopped still, terrified. But as the footsteps approached, he heard the voice change. 'Oh, it's Richards, isn't it? Come from the Rectory to help in the kitchen?'

Daniel nodded and dared to look up. A tall man in black was looking down at him; his face was thin and bony, with a hooked red nose. He looked, not so much unkind as permanently busy, with no time to think of kind words for anyone. 'Be quick now, boy. Go round the back to the kitchen and Mrs Simpson will tell you what's to be done, and mind you call me *Mr* Simpson!' The last words were uttered sternly, as if Daniel had already been cheeky enough to call this man by his first name.

'Please, sir, are you the butler, Mr Simpson?' asked Daniel.

''Course I am, boy, and mind you remember it. Now be quick!'

The kitchen door at the Manor was twice the size of the one at the Rectory, and Daniel stared round in awe. Nobody noticed him for a moment: maids were rushing to and fro, and it seemed that an army of cooks were beating mixtures in bowls or chopping at tables, all around the room.

Out of habit he made his way across to the stove. This one was longer than his own stove, and with a more complicated arrangement of ovens and hot water taps. Pans let out great billowing clouds of steam on top, and there was a delicious smell of roasting meat from inside. The warmth made Daniel feel more at ease. He stood next to the stove waiting for someone to notice him . . . and for a second he became confused. This stove, this warmth, so like another . . . and why was he here? He started to recall. What purpose was there in this haunting, this taking one soul out of its own time and into another? He gripped the rail along the front of the stove for support, trying to remember something, to remember . . . faces, loving faces, his parents . . . But as quickly as the glimmering had come it disappeared again, leaving him blank and dizzy.

'What? Is the child sick?' It was a young woman's voice. 'Not much use to us if he is, with all those boots to be polished.' The second voice was gloomy, as if it knew of all the troubles of this world and beyond.

Two maids were staring down at him, but they were quickly elbowed to one side by a fat and motherly woman who was clearly in charge. Her face was round and her forearms, where she had rolled up his sleeves, were as strong and gnarled as tree trunks.

'Richards-from-the-Rectory, you've been lent to us to work, not daydream,' she said, with an amused look in her eye. 'I'm Mrs Simpson, and I'm the housekeeper, and you probably met my husband outside on his way out.'

'I did, Mrs . . .'

'Now, Lizzie here will take you out into the back corridor and there's a pile of boots and shoes want cleaning, and so I wouldn't waste any time. When this house is full it's a powerful lot of work for the likes of us.' And she rushed off across the kitchen, the huge bunch of keys clanking at her waist.

Lizzie, the one who had spoken in such a gloomy voice, led him into the chilly passage where he sat on the cold stone floor and started work cleaning the row of boots of all shapes and sizes.

A little while later, he wandered along to one of the many back entrances to the huge house, stretching his arms and back after being hunched over his work. The door was slightly ajar, and a chill draught blew in. Daniel was about to close it when he heard voices talking outside

80

– men's voices. They were low and secretive, and so he froze with his hand on the doorknob, listening.

'It's tonight, then?' said the first man.

'Ay, but only about seven of us at the most. Samuel says we must be careful who we do trust.'

'The word is being carried all round the parish. By the time this month's out I'll lay we'll have a full Society. Then the masters 'ull have to listen.'

The second man made a small note of doubt in his throat: 'Well, I'm not too sure of that, Harry. It won't be too easy to change their minds; and don't forget, if it goes against us, our wages 'ull be put down and there'll be nothing we can do.'

'Not with Samuel Smith leading us,' said the first man, with great pride in his voice. 'You see, tonight, Thomas; you'll see how it'll be.'

'Seven o'clock then, at Samuel's house?'

'Yes, but not a word to anyone, not even to your wife, man!'

Daniel heard a trundling noise then, as if a wheelbarrow was being pushed along the cinder path. Then, as the noise of feet in heavy boots faded, there was silence.

'What can be going to happen?' Daniel wondered to himself. Two things were certain: first, that whatever it was they were planning at Samuel's house, George would be there; and second, that he had to find out what was going on, although he was not sure why he felt that so strongly. It went beyond mere curiosity. He felt convinced he had a *job* to do.

The day passed very slowly indeed, although he was kept busy all the time. He could not help contrasting the kindly Mrs Simpson, as round and plump and rosy as her husband was tall and scrawny, with the bad-tempered Mrs Brennan at the Rectory. The kitchen at the Manor was a happy place. But at odd times during the day he thought he noticed some of the women whispering. Most of them were married to the Squire's farmworkers; clearly they knew, or suspected, that their husbands were becoming involved in something which made them glance over their shoulders nervously, and speak in low voices.

When it had been dark for quite some time, Daniel looked up at the great wooden clock on the kitchen wall. It meant nothing to him, for he could no more tell the time than he could read, but he guessed from the day's routine that it must be nearly seven o'clock. The dinner was about to be served; the kitchen was filled with delicious smells, and the maids had been clattering the china in the huge walk-in cupboard that led off one side of the room. Mrs Simpson had told him to take a piece of bread and a bowl of broth, and noticed now that instead of eating he was staring at the clock.

'Why, bless you, boy, are you wanting to go somewhere? Are you late?' One or two of the other women laughed, and a girl called out; 'The lad's goin' courtin', I'll be bound.'

Daniel blushed crimson, and asked, 'Oh, Mrs Simpson, what time is it?'

'It's a quarter to seven; and why would you want to know?'

Daniel hesitated, 'Er . . . because the Reverend said I was to bring my own bed here, and I forgot it, Ma'am. So I thought that if my work's done, I could run back home and get it before Mrs Brennan locks the kitchen door.' He held his breath and waited for her reply.

'Well,' she said dubiously, 'we were going to make you up a bed in the groom's bedroom.'

'But I always sleep next to the stove, Mrs Simpson, and that way I can make sure all's well first thing in the morning.'

'Very well, then.'

Daniel let out his breath.

'But be sure you don't dawdle; and you can take my good wishes to Mrs Brennan whilst you're there.'

In a minute Daniel had jumped up and rushed out, leaving the maids to stare with astonishment at his half-finished food.

There was a bright moon sailing through wispy clouds, illuminating the Manor garden with its pale, ghostly light. Daniel ran silently along; he had left his boots behind for the sake of speed and silence, and his feet soon became so cold they hardly felt the rough ground. He ran along beside walls and hedges, so that if anyone were to be talking in Winterstoke that night they would not notice him in the shadows. But there was no one in sight; the little cottages had closed doors, and hardly any light could escape through the chinks in the sacking hung at the windows. It was utterly silent.

Samuel Smith's cottage was at the other end of the straggling village. Daniel hurried; he did not want to be too late. When he reached the forge he paused. He could see two men ahead of him who slowed down, and knocked at Smith's door, looking stealthily around. Daniel shrank back, in case they should see him, but the door closed again behind them, and he went on. Reaching the cottage, he slipped around the side. All the windows were covered; there was no chance of seeing into the downstairs room. Unless . . . he noticed a square of light above him, at a strange little window high up in the side wall. It must have been put there to let air circulate during the summer, when the cottages all became as hot as they were cold in the winter. The hot air would rise, so sometimes the labourers would knock a small hole high up, to help the ventilation. Of course, because this was Samuel Smith's home, the window was well constructed. But it was well over six feet above the ground and must be only about ten inches below the low ceiling of the room.

Daniel looked around. He could hear the low murmur of voices from inside, and was filled with a desperate desire to see what was happening.

Samuel's wheelbarrow lay near by, but it would surely move if he stood on it, unless . . . Quickly he pulled it over and wedged sticks and stones all round the front wheel so that it would not budge. Then he found an old wooden box, which Samuel was probably going to use for fire-wood, and wedged it securely in the centre of the wheelbarrow, packing more twigs around it to make it steady. Everything seemed to make a crashing noise in the silence, but nobody came out. Then, very carefully, he climbed over the side of the wheelbarrow and on to the box, steadying himself against the side wall of the house. Raising himself on his toes for a little extra height, he peeped in through the window, which no one had bothered to cover because it was so small.

The first thing he saw – in the room lit with eerily

flickering candlelight – gave him such a shock that he nearly fell off his perch: it was a skeleton! Looming out of the shadows at the side of the Smiths' fireplace was a horrible grinning skeleton, which made Daniel's knees tremble. He closed his eyes for a second and looked again. As he did, a man passed in front of the thing and it moved slightly in the breeze of his passing. Daniel sighed with relief. It was only a picture on a huge piece of paper, pinned up to Samuel Smith's wall. The Smiths' table had clearly been pulled out of its usual position and stood in front of the skeleton with a large open book on it.

'It must be the Bible,' Daniel thought. He could not see much of the room from where he stood, but it seemed full of people whose shadows made dark patterns on the floor, and who moved about with slow and solemn paces, as if according to a mysterious plan.

Suddenly Samuel Smith came into his line of vision and stood behind the table, by the Bible, with a man on either side of him Daniel had never seen before. Samuel was holding a piece of paper, which he studied rather nervously, and his face was very serious indeed. He seemed to be reading words from the paper; Daniel could only catch the low murmur of his voice, but could not hear exactly what he was saying. Then five men marched forward from the part of the room where they had been hidden from Daniel's sight, and stood with their hands clasped behind them in front of the table. Because they had their backs to Daniel, he could not see their faces, but even if he had he would not have been able to recognize them. For each of the five men who stood there with heads bowed had a broad white bandage around his eyes, blindfolding him completely.

Daniel felt puzzled, but worried too. He knew that whatever was happening in Samuel Smith's house had something to do with the warning pinned to the Winterstoke Oak – with something that was forbidden. An oath – didn't people swear oaths on the Bible? The thought made his knees tremble, so that for a second he found it hard to keep his balance. When he was steady again, he peered down into the room once more. Samuel was reading out words from the paper, and then each man seemed to repeat them. By straining his ears he could just catch odd phrases, because the labourers in front of the table spoke very slowly and distinctly, as if they were speaking a foreign language. He heard the words 'God' and 'I solemnly do vow', and then the bandages were removed, and one of the men with Samuel pointed to the skeleton – as if he were asking the six men to learn a lesson from it. Then each man replaced his own bandage and more words were said. It seemed to go on for a long time and Daniel's feet felt numb. The low murmuring and the flickering light in the room annoyed him now, like a foolish game played by children he knew, but which he had not been invited to join in.

Then, to his astonishment, Joe Smith walked forward and led each man in turn forward to the Bible, holding his hand on it as Samuel said words for the man to repeat. 'So, Joe's in this too,' Daniel thought, full of envy and admiration for the older boy. Joe's face looked more mature – as if the seriousness of the occasion had changed him from a boy into a man.

At last it was all over. Samuel lit two more candles on the table so that more light flared into the room. The men still stood with their backs to Daniel, but took off their bandages and shook hands with each other, and with the two strangers. And as they moved around the room, Daniel could at last see their faces. He recognized William Fletcher, whose poor cottage he had visited, and with him another of Mr Winterton's farmworkers, a man called James Brown, who was famous in the district for his strength. Two of Squire Plumptree's workers, the ones he had overheard that morning, Harry Eades and Thomas Leggat, were talking quietly to one of the strangers. But it was the last man, the man who started to fold up the pile of bandages neatly, so that his sister would not return to find her house untidy – it was that man whose face made Daniel's heart leap. For the man now smiling and clapping Samuel on the shoulders with a glow of triumph on his face was, of course, George Wright.

Chapter 9

THE SPY

More notices appeared in Winterstoke, nailed to trees and gateposts, and they stayed there too as the men hurried by, not even stopping to look. Even if they could not read, they knew now what the notice said, and so every man in the parish chose to ignore it. There was a suppressed excitement in the village, and even the oldest women were aware of it – shaking their heads and warning that 'No good will come.' Daniel heard it everywhere – in the kitchen at the Manor House, and back at the Rectory and in the village street too. People whispered about the new Friendly Society, and how within the month all the men would belong.

Daniel did not dare tell George that he had watched the first secret ceremony. He could guess what his friend would say, and felt partly ashamed himself for peering through the chink like a spy. But he wanted to talk to George, to ask him what it all meant, and it was hard without giving himself away. So he said nothing.

Three days after the night of the ceremony, when the Squire's visitors had departed and Daniel was back at the Rectory, George came into the kitchen. Daniel was scouring the kitchen table as usual since Mrs Brennan was particularly fussy that it should be done every day. So he bent to the task, whilst George stood silently, looking down at him.

'Seems to me you've grown very silent of late, Dan,' said George at last.

'Me? Oh no, George.' He carried on scrubbing.

'Are we not friends any more, lad?'

''Course we are. What do you mean?' Daniel did not look up from his task.

A huge hand reached over his shoulder and took the scrubbing brush from him, throwing it angrily into the tin pail so that some water splashed on the floor.

'Will you stop doing that, and talk to me!' said George, angry now.

To Daniel's horror, tears came into his eyes, and he bent his head so that George would not see. He could not bear to have a secret from his friend, and yet he could not bear to tell him the truth. George stared at him. 'For pity's sake, lad, tell me what's the matter!'

Daniel dashed a hand roughly across his eyes. 'George, what's going to happen? In the village, I mean.'

'It seems to me that you must be talking about the Society,' George said, more gently now. 'Look lad, it's no secret, really. The village folk know – but the gentry don't, and that's the way we have to keep it. For the time being, at least.'

'Are you . . . are you in it, George?' Daniel asked, nervously.

'That's not for you to know, Dan. It wouldn't do you no good to know either way,' George said seriously. 'Look, my lad, you're like family to me, you know that, don't you?' Daniel nodded miserably. 'Well then, I think I was wrong to talk to you as I did, about the wrongs I see all round me, because you're still only a boy, and there's time enough for you to be thinking of such matters.'

'But I do think of them, George – now,' Daniel protested. 'I want to talk to you about such things, I want to be like Joe.'

'My nephew's fifteen, Dan, and he's worked on the Squire's land in all weathers since he was ten. He's a man now.'

'Is he in the Society?' Daniel blurted out, terrified as soon as he had spoken.

George frowned. 'That's not the kind of question anyone in this village asks anyone else,' he said sternly. 'And listen to me, Daniel. If you hear anything, if you see anything, you keep your mouth tight shut – is that clear?'

Daniel nodded silently, but felt rebellious. Why should he be kept out of George's confidence? Suddenly he felt jealous of Joe Smith, who worked in the fields like a man, instead of being tied to a stupid kitchen and a stove like the maids and the cooks. He kicked the table leg angrily, but still said nothing.

The kitchen clock ticked. They could hear Dorothea

Forster playing the piano, and the shouts of Henry, James and Frederick as they played in the garden. There was a gentle hiss of steam from the potatoes which simmered on top of the stove, and a tantalizing smell of meat from inside it. Soon Mrs Brennan and Annie would come in, and this moment would be lost for ever. He wanted to tell George . . . but what? It was impossible for Daniel to rid himself of his impulse to warn. *But there's nothing we can do to change things.*

All he knew was that he cared about this tall young man beside him, whose smock smelt strongly of manure. So he reached out and put a hand on George's arm. 'You'll be careful, won't you, George?' he said.

George patted the hand with his own huge, dirty one: 'Ay, laddie, bless you. I'll be careful. And soon I promise I *will* explain it all to you.' Then, with a grin, he bent to pick up the scrubbing brush from the pail of filthy water, handing it to Daniel with a flourish: 'This is yours, I think, young master!' And then he went out.

Lunch had been served to the family and cleared away again, and Daniel was sitting to eat potatoes, carrots and gravy, when Annie came in. 'Daniel,' she said breathlessly, 'the master do want you. In the study.'

Mrs Brennan looked sternly across the table at him. 'I hope you haven't been doing anything wrong, you rascal, or you'll be in more trouble from me.'

'I done nothing, Mrs Brennan,' protested Daniel, wiping his mouth with the back of his hand and jumping up.

To his surprise, Mrs Forster was in the study with her embroidery. She was a pale, thin woman who was often ill, and spent most days lying on the chaise-longue in the drawing-room whilst her oldest daughter, Dorothea, read to her. The Rector's sons were always being told to be quiet because their mother had a headache, and once Henry had whispered to Daniel that it was a confounded nuisance. But Daniel felt sorry for the mistress; he liked to catch glimpses of her as she trailed about in her pretty shawls, smelling of lavender; for she was what he imagined a mother to be like – a delicate china ornament you could not touch in case it broke in your hands. By now he had no memory of *another* kind of mother – someone brisk and jolly who could do anything from paint a picture to put up shelves. That mother's image had faded completely, had drifted away into the blackness, leaving Daniel alone.

Mrs Forster looked up when Daniel entered the room and smiled her gentle, tired smile. 'Ah, it's Richards. Come here, my boy, and make yourself comfortable.' She pointed towards a footstool near the fire.

Daniel stared at her. He had never before been asked to sit in the presence of the master and mistress; it seemed wrong to him.

The Rector was standing by the window. 'Sit down, lad,' he said in a hearty, loud voice, that made Daniel jump after Mrs Forster's soothing tones. So Daniel crossed the room and sat nervously on the edge of the stool, looking around the dark, richly decorated room and wondering what they wanted with him.

'Now, Daniel,' said the Reverend Forster, taking a seat just across the room from where he sat, 'you've been with us a long time, haven't you?'

'As long as I can remember, sir.'

'I'm sure you are grateful, Daniel, that my husband took you in out of charity, and his Christian duty,' added Mrs Forster, her fingers moving smoothly at their work.

'I am, to be sure I am, Ma'am,' said Daniel, as the warm firelight made him feel relaxed. He added, with great feeling: 'I *am* very grateful to you, sir.'

'Good, good.' The Rector folded his arms, and looked on Daniel kindly. Then he nodded to his wife. 'You see, my dear, this boy is a loyal boy. And I know I could trust him to tell me if he knew of anything that might harm his benefactor, or offend against God.'

'I am sure Daniel is worthy of your faith, husband,' said Mrs Forster, gazing at Daniel with such a mild, yet searching gaze that he felt himself flushing. What did they mean? Why had they asked him in here, to sit him down and talk to him of gratitude? They were looking at him as though expecting an answer, so he mumbled, 'You can trust me, sir.'

The Reverend Forster rubbed his hands. 'Good, good,' he said again, and then fell silent for a moment, scratching his nose as if he was unsure of how to go on. Then he cleared his throat. 'Daniel, some days ago now a man came to this house, to meet with some local gentlemen and myself. Do you know that man?'

'Samuel Smith, sir.'

'The very one. Do you like that man, Daniel?'

'Mr Smith is much respected, sir. He is the best man on the Squire's estate, and a good man, too.'

'A Methodist preacher, I hear,' said Mrs Forster lightly.

'Such men can inflame the hearts and minds of people, although not always for good purposes,' said the Rector, frowning, so that Daniel quailed, wondering what he was supposed to say.

'What do you think, boy?' asked the Rector sharply.

Daniel lowered his head. 'I'm sure I don't know about such matters, sir.'

'Maybe not.' There was another short silence. Then Mr Forster stood up suddenly, making Daniel jump. He towered over the boy and said in his gravest voice: 'Now listen to me, Daniel. I will ask you a question, as your benefactor, and I expect you to give me an honest Christian answer, for the sake of your life in this household and all the favours which, for the grace of God, you have received from my family. Is that clear?' Daniel nodded.

'Well then, tell me if you know of any secret society that is being formed in this village, with unholy oaths upon the Holy Bible – oaths of the kind that should only be made in the presence of a Minister of God? Do you know of any such thing in my parish?'

The fire seemed very hot. Daniel's head whirled as he sat there, and he felt sweat trickle down the side of his body. He realized now why the Rector's wife was there, and why they had let him sit down. Looking up, he saw her earnest, questioning eyes fixed on him, and he could not bear it.

'No, sir,' he said, praying silently to be forgiven for his lie.

'Are you sure of that? I know you are acquainted with the people of the parish. Did you not visit the home of

Samuel Smith with Wright, a little while ago?' It was because the Rector's voice was quiet and persuasive that Daniel found it so difficult; he wished he would be stern and angry instead.

'Yes, sir. Mary Smith is George's sister. We went for a bite of supper.'

'And have you ever heard Smith utter words of rebellion against his station in life, and in particular against his master, Squire Plumptree?'

'No, sir.'

'I hope that you are telling the truth, Daniel, for you know the good Lord watches night and day and hears the lies we utter,' said Mrs Forster.

'I am telling the truth, I swear it,' Daniel said staunchly, looking her in the face, yet reddening despite himself.

'I believe you, boy,' the Rector said, with conviction. 'You may go now, but be sure to tell me if you do hear anything, will you not, for the sake of your great obligation to me?'

As Daniel nodded he added, 'And I wish you to take a message to the Manor later today, at nightfall when the Squire will be back from hunting. I will give the envelope to Annie for you to carry.' Daniel nodded again, bowed his head and fled from the room.

A couple of hours later when it was already dark, Annie came to him carrying a small envelope. 'The master said to take this and deliver it to Mr Plumptree,' she said, 'and be sure to deliver it into his own hands, and no one else's.'

'Have you seen George, Annie?' asked Daniel.

'No, not since dinner time when he passed by.'

'Is he coming to see you tonight, then, to take you walking?' Daniel's voice was teasing, and the girl blushed.

'No – he is not, young man, not that it's your business! George said he's going to Samuel Smith's at seven o'clock sharp.' She stopped and put a hand quickly to her mouth. 'But mind you don't tell nobody.'

Walking to the Manor House along the muddy lane Daniel felt thoughtful. Although the Manor was quite close to the Rectory it was placed so that you could not approach it directly, but only by a roundabout route of intersecting lanes. The direct route was across fields, through the bare spiky hedges. Daniel decided not to hurry, for the Rector's questions had shaken him badly. He wanted time to think. This was very serious; or why was George going to Samuel Smith's again, without telling him? It must be another secret meeting.

Daniel turned the Rector's letter over and over in his hands. It was small and stiff, with the Squire's name written in slanting black marks on the front. Behind – the Rector's seal, a messy blob of red wax, which looked as though it had been done in a great hurry. What could it say? Why would his master be sending an urgent message to the Manor at this time? Daniel thought it must have something to do with Samuel Smith and the men – but then, *everything* in the village seemed to revolve around their activities, and there seemed to be secrets behind every door. Again he fingered the envelope; it was no use thinking about opening it, for he would have to find someone who could read. That was it! He must take it to George . . .

But he stopped in his tracks with horror at the thought.

To betray his master, and break open the seal of his private letter! No – that was something no honest boy could do, not even if his life depended on it. And in any case, it might be a letter on church business, it might be anything at all . . . Daniel felt miserable suddenly at the series of events which made everyone suspicious of everything, and which made close friends keep things from each other. Like George. Here he was, off to Samuel Smith's again, despite all the warnings on the village trees. Why could he not take Daniel fully into his confidence? At least the Rector trusted him – or at least, *seemed* to trust him. Daniel sighed. There it was again – the old doubt; the feeling that nobody was what they seemed.

Just as Daniel reached the place where two lanes met and crossed, he heard voices, and saw the glimmer of a lantern. Without thinking, he shrank back into the darkness of the hedge. The voices came closer; they belonged to two men.

'All right then, George, I'll be off,' said the first, and Daniel recognized the voice of Harry Eades.

'You won't be late, Harry?' said George with gruff seriousness. 'For a lot will depend on this night's work.'

'I know that, right enough. It'll be just us five then, with the Smiths?' said the other man.

'Aye, but we'll be making up our minds once for all, as to who we have, and how we may all act next.'

'I say we should all meet on the Green, and be damned with all this hiding,' said Harry Eades with a flash of anger.

'I agree, man. What can they do to a whole village? Any

97

road, we'll decide tonight, but I think you and I and Brown should tell Samuel that we're not afraid.'

'That we aren't.'

There was a silence for a few seconds; Daniel scarcely dared to breathe. The letter burned in his hand. Then George spoke again. 'I'd best hurry along, Harry. I've to clear the bakehouse first – and it would fall on this night.'

'Don't worry, George, you'll have time, and I'm along to visit my old mother now in any case. So I'll see you later . . .'

Daniel listened to their footsteps until they ceased. Then he continued on his way, his feeling of unease growing stronger. Once he reached the Manor drive he hesitated. Should he go to the kitchen door? Annie had said he was to deliver the letter into the Squire's own hand. But he could not possibly walk up to the grand front door by himself. The building dwarfed him; he felt suddenly helpless.

Deciding to find Mr Simpson to ask his advice, Daniel turned at last down the side path that led around the back of the large building to the servants' door. Golden light slanted from tall, brightly-lit windows above him, making squared patterns on the gravel path. And as he rounded a jutting bay window, Daniel saw something that made his blood freeze and his heart beat wildly – something he understood quite clearly as soon as he saw it.

There on the path stood Squire Plumptree himself, in his high polished boots and starched white neckcloth, talking to a man who wore the rough clothes of a labourer. Daniel recognized him at once – it was Thomas Leggat, one of the men whom Daniel had seen at the secret

98

ceremony. Why would the Squire stand talking secretly in the cold darkness to a mere farmworker unless . . . ? Daniel started to shiver.

The man glanced round nervously as he spoke, his eyes glinting in the light from the window like those of an animal at bay. The Squire had a peculiar look of pleasure on his face – not the kind that comes from happiness, but the kind which stems from black, grim satisfaction, as when a hated opponent has been defeated. Daniel strained his ears to hear.

'. . . and so all is arranged, and I suggest to you that you keep yourself indoors,' the Squire was saying.

'Aye, master,' mumbled Leggat.

'That will be all then . . . Oh, and here's payment for you.' The Squire reached into his waistcoat pocket and brought out a coin which glinted brightly in the warm light from the window, and which Thomas Leggat almost snatched, so great was his haste to hurry it into his pocket.

At that moment – he could not help it – Daniel sneezed. Both men whirled round.

'Who's hiding there, in the name of God?' called the Squire in a furious voice.

Daniel stepped forward into the light. 'It's only me, your worship, with a letter from my master.' He held out the small envelope. 'He said I were to give it into no hands but your own, sir. So I was going to find Mr Simpson to ask him to lead me to you, sir.' He spoke in his slowest, most ignorant voice.

'Hmmmmff, it's only the Rector's kitchen boy. Well, give the letter here, lad!'

As Leggat and Daniel stood in silence watching, Squire Plumptree tore open the envelope and read its contents quickly. When he had finished he shook his head, and uttered an odd, triumphant grunt. He muttered – half to himself, and half to Leggat – as he thrust the paper into his coat pocket, 'I knew you'd have no stomach for it, Reverend – not in the end. But 'tis too late now, too late . . .'

Leggat coughed with embarrassment, and jerked his head in Daniel's direction. Squire Plumptree glared at him: 'You can be off now, Leggat, and be sure you mind about the state of the hedges and the meadow gate!' His voice was false and harsh. The man touched his forelock, and melted away into the darkness.

'Please, sir, may I go too, sir?' Daniel asked, itching to run through the village and find George, to warn him of what he had seen. Thomas Leggat . . . he must have told the Squire about the meetings. And what was going to happen that the Rector did not want to happen?

'Maybe I'll go inside to pen a reply to your master, for you to take back with you,' murmured the Squire.

Daniel shuffled his feet in desperation. *Hurry up, hurry!* he thought, knowing that he could not go until dismissed. He could almost hear the minutes ticking by on the great gold watch that was tucked into the Squire's waistcoat pocket, its broad chain stretched across his stomach. The waiting was intolerable, and still Squire Plumptree just stood there, deep in thought.

'Mmmm,' he grunted to himself, 'maybe it's better for him to know nothing, after all . . .' He looked up at Daniel, speaking in his normal voice: 'You, lad, you can go now.

Tell your master I . . . no, just tell him there was no reply, and I will call on him in the morning. Now be off!'

Daniel did not need telling twice. He turned and ran along the side of the house, out into the front and down the long, dark drive. He was free! He could get there in time . . .

Just as he reached the gates, however, a figure stepped out from the deeper blackness which encircled them, a figure which had been hiding in the thick bushes by the Manor entrance. It was a man – a tall man who reached out a strong, bony hand which gripped Daniel painfully by the neck. He wriggled but the grip tightened – viciously. And then a rough voice growled, 'Now my young master, my little listener, I be wanting you to tell me where you're rushing off to, like.' The tone was low and menacing, and as Daniel recognized it, his knees seemed to turn to water. It was Thomas Leggat – the man he now knew to be a spy.

Chapter 10

HUNTED

For a few seconds Daniel froze with horror. He had lost all power to move or cry out; all he was conscious of was the pressure of Thomas Leggat's fingers digging into his arm. Then he struggled to free himself, but the man only gripped him all the more firmly and gave a short, unpleasant laugh.

'Oh . . . so you want a fight, do you? We'll soon see about that, young sir!'

'Let . . . me . . . go,' panted Daniel, in pain now.

'I'll teach you to listen in on talk what don't concern you,' Leggat said in a low, threatening voice.

'I wasn't listening. I didn't hear nothing. Honest!' Daniel protested. He relaxed a little in Leggat's grasp, realizing that the sure way to make someone suspect you is to struggle. And as he let his body go limp, he felt those cruel fingers slacken their hold just a fraction.

'Oh yes, you didn't hear, hey? And how can I be sure of that, Master Richards?'

'I'm telling you. I just came to give my master's letter, and that's all! I swear to God, mister!'

He had made his voice as stupid and vacant as possible, and could almost read Leggat's thoughts as he wondered whether to believe this dim kitchen boy.

'You know how good I am with my sickle, Master Richards?' he whispered at last, in an evil voice.

Daniel gulped. 'I . . . er . . . don't know nothin', sir.'

'Oh, you don't, hey? Well, you should know. You should know that I've got a mighty sharp sickle what I use to slice off the ears of boys what listen to others talkin'. You should know that my sickle is partickerly partial to the throats of kitchen boys, because they're nice and plump, see?'

Daniel went quite cold with terror as he felt something sharp prick the side of his neck. A small, frightened sound escaped from his throat, and it must have pleased Leggat – for he suddenly let out a coarse, triumphant laugh. And just for that second, fear gave Daniel strength. He kicked out viciously, and his clumsy boot caught the man's knee cap so that he howled with sudden pain and rage.

In a flash Daniel had broken free, and started to run – out through the Manor gates, and along the first bit of lane. He knew that Leggat would only take a moment or two to recover and then would be after him. His long legs would certainly overtake Daniel's short ones, and then . . .

Daniel knew he could not possibly be lucky enough to escape a second time, and he had to warn George. He must tell George and Samuel Smith that there had been a spy at their meeting, someone who had certainly sold his information to Squire Plumptree. The warning on the oak seemed dreadful now.

'Come back here, you little devil! Wait till I . . .' Leggat's voice faded, and Daniel heard him start to run. He would easily catch up, unless . . . Then Daniel thought of a plan. It would waste a few seconds, but might throw the man off his scent.

There was no stile, nor gate, nor any other kind of opening into the field along this stretch of lane, but Daniel remembered that the hedgerow was unusually thin and straggly. So, like a small burrowing animal, he dived at it, scrabbling wildly at the twigs and branches. A thorn tore his face and his hair was dragged but he took no notice. In a second he had forced his way through and lay panting on the cold, damp bank on the other side. Warm blood trickled down his face from a cut.

Footsteps sounded along the lane. Then they stopped. Leggat was listening, and Daniel held his breath. He thought his heartbeat was so loud that Leggat must hear it, and would follow its thuds to the hiding place. In the darkness he fancied he could hear the man breathing just a few feet away, and he knew now how small hunted creatures must feel as they cringe, paralysed with fear, waiting for the hunter.

Leggat cursed. 'Damn him!' and spat into the lane. Which way would he go now? If he went back to the Manor, Daniel could remove his boots and tiptoe along the lane. But if he stayed there . . . Daniel sent up a fervent prayer that the man would go.

He did, but not far enough. Retracing his steps about forty yards towards the Manor, Thomas Leggat stopped again. Silence. 'He must be squatting down and waiting for me to move,' thought Daniel. And all the time, the Squire knew – but what? And what would he do? '*I must get to George*,' said Daniel to himself, with a greater sense of urgency than he had ever experienced in his life.

There was only one thing to do. Very carefully, he untied the laces of his big, old boots, and eased them off. Hardly daring to breathe, he inched them behind him, placing them at the foot of the hedge. 'I'll come back for 'em in the morning, if I live through this night,' he thought – and it was not until next day that he remembered how oddly concerned he had been for his boots, and at such a time.

Then he set off gingerly across the rough ground, ploughed ready for some winter crop, but stony and uneven. He kept his head down from instinct, even though no one could have seen him in that darkness. He had worked out that if he traced a straight course across the field he should reach the churchyard wall on the far corner. Then he could climb into the graveyard, cross it, and creep along the lane to the Rectory. George had said he had to clean out the bakehouse oven; he might not yet have left.

It was hard to sense the right direction. Many times Daniel stumbled and fell, biting back the cry that rose to his lips. His feet were numb; he noticed no pain now. When he was about halfway across the field the moon broke from behind clouds, and he saw in that instant that he should change his course slightly to the right. But the light which helped him might also betray him, and he glanced fearfully over one shoulder – expecting a cry and pursuit. No one called, and there was no sign of Leggat, yet Daniel could not afford to slacken his pace. Rather did he increase it, so great was his sense of time running out.

When he finally reached the low drystone wall which separated the Squire's field from his church, Daniel was panting loudly. As he hurled himself at the wall, he grazed his hands and feet, and tore his fingernails, but barely noticed. His breathing was like fire; his heart pounded.

He jumped down at last on the other side and his feet rested on something very different from the rough, stony soil. It was cold and smooth. Daniel looked down and shuddered. He was standing on a flat, white marble slab which glimmered at him like a moth's wing in the fitful moonlight. All around him were similar tombstones, some flat, some standing, some grand, some small and simple, some decorated with carved angels and urns – all marking the last resting places of those who had lived in Winterstoke before him.

Daniel felt a cry of superstitious fear rise in his mouth, and clapped his own hand across to suppress it. He jumped off the slab as though it were burning his feet. Everyone knows it is bad luck to walk on graves – Daniel had always believed that, and never, not in his wildest dreams of bravery, would he have ventured into Winterstoke churchyard at night, and alone.

His teeth were chattering but he took a deep breath and

stilled them. It was no use being cowardly, no use drawing back now. Besides – he thought, with a quick, unexpected feeling of amusement – the ghosts in the churchyard (if there were such things) were bound to be a lot friendlier than the man Thomas Leggat who might still be lurking along Manor Lane. So he picked his way around the tombstones, trying to stop his imagination from hearing sounds and seeing movements in the darker shadows around the church.

Soon the iron gates clicked shut behind him. Daniel summoned all his failing strength to run up the steep hill to the Rectory, stumbling over his own bruised feet, until at last he reached the shelter of those familiar walls.

Annie and Mrs Brennan were sitting at the kitchen table eating their evening meal. The family must have already been served; that meant it must be seven o'clock already.

'Where's George, Annie?' Daniel gasped.

Mrs Brennan frowned. 'That's no way to come bursting into my kitchen, Richards. I'll thank you to mind –'

'*Please*, Mrs Brennan, tell me where George is!'

Something in his voice made the cook stop, and the two women stared at him in astonishment. 'He's out in the bakehouse, Dan'l,' said Annie, and added, 'He were told to see to the chimney in time for tomorrow's baking, and it put him in a dreadful temper, on account of he said he'd be late for something. He's about to go now, I'd think.'

The bakehouse was a low outbuilding, approached through a door at the rear of the scullery. It dated from the time before there was a stove in the Rectory kitchen, when all the food would have been cooked on the open fire, as it still was in the cottages. Then, once or twice a week the bread would be baked in the stone bakehouse oven – as Mrs Brennan, who believed in old-fashioned methods, still did. But the chimney often grew blocked, so that the room would fill with smoke, and then George would have to clear it before next baking day.

There he was, in the act of tying on his kerchief, the job finished. He looked surprised to see Daniel, who gasped, 'George, I've got to talk to you.'

'Not now, lad. I'm late. Mary's expecting me for a bite o' supper.' Daniel heard the lie, and winced that his friend could not be honest with him, even now.

'George, you've got to listen to me, you've got to, *please*!'

Hearing the desperation in that shout, George looked worried. 'What is it, laddie, what's wrong?'

With his words falling over each other, Daniel blurted out the full story, starting from the Rector's questions and ending with Leggat's sickle, or knife, held at his throat. George's face grew dark with anger. But his first anger was not against Leggat, it was against Daniel himself. 'What you haven't said is how you know Thomas Leggat is one of us. Have you been following me?'

Tears filled Daniel's eyes; he could not bear it. 'Please, George, don't . . . not now. Well, yes I have! But it was only because I wanted to be with you, George. Whatever you do, I want to do! And anyway, if I hadn't I wouldn't have been able to warn you . . . just as we should be warning Samuel Smith now!'

George looked down, as if he were ashamed. 'All right, lad,' he said gruffly, 'I'll go off to Samuel's now and you'd better not follow me, Dan'l. It might not be safe.'

Daniel stared at him. There were just a few seconds to make up his mind and act on the sudden surge of conviction inside him. He must not let George go; he did not know why, but he just *knew*. He sensed danger, just as an animal can sense things out of sight which threaten its life. Something dreadful was about to happen, and he knew he had to keep George away. '*There's nothing we can do to change things* . . . But, oh yes there is,' he thought.

He backed away from George. With a false note of good cheer in his voice he called out, 'All right then, George, I'll go and have a bite to eat.' And instantly he was out of the door and turning the key in the lock behind him. There was no other way out. George was a prisoner.

As he ran back through the scullery he could hear George's fists start to beat against the old, thick door. But it was much too far away from the rest of the house for the Rector or his family to hear. And Daniel stood still in front of Annie and Mrs Brennan, wondering at his own daring.

They stared up at him, and he felt older in their eyes – as if he had grown up during that run through the darkness. 'Please don't ask me to tell you why, not yet. But I've locked George in the bakehouse. He were going to get into trouble – real, bad trouble, Annie. If you care for him, don't let him out, d'you hear me? I'll tell you about it when I'm back. And . . . I'm sorry, Mrs Brennan, ma'am.' Amazed, the women said nothing at all, as he ran from the kitchen.

Now it seemed to him that this night had been a long nightmare of fleeing through blackness, not knowing what enemies might be lurking behind the next hedge. His bare feet made a light, pattering sound along the lane; Winterstoke was totally still. He began to feel pleased and confident. He would get to Samuel's house in time, and they would all listen to him with respect. The men would all leave quietly, and then Samuel Smith and Joe would shake his hand, and tell him he had done well. The thought made him puff out his chest; and he slackened his pace a fraction.

But as he reached the narrow track that led up past the forge, Daniel sensed danger once more. He heard voices ahead, and dived for the shelter of the walls, slinking along like a mouse. There was a man ahead – no, two or three men, and with a lantern. Inch by inch he crept forward after them, until he could see Samuel Smith's door.

The loud rat-tat of the knocking rang out in the stillness. There was no reply, so it was repeated, more fiercely this time. And at last, very slowly, the cottage door opened.

Samuel Smith stood on the threshold, tall and dignified in his working smock, with his arms folded across his chest. For a few minutes he simply gazed in silence at the men on his doorstep, then just nodded at them, as if accepting in advance whatever it was they had to say. It was almost as if – Daniel thought with wonder – he were expecting them.

The tallest man stepped forward, and Daniel recognized him in the lantern's rays. It was the parish constable, John Hale, and he spoke out loudly and slowly, as if he had carefully memorized the words: 'I have a warrant from the Magistrate for your arrest, Mr Smith.'

'For me?' Samuel's voice was quiet.

'Yes, and for others beside you. For whatever men I find to be in your house this night. You are charged with giving and receiving an unlawful oath. You must come along with me.'

'Where to?' asked Samuel, as the other men in the cottage crowded round him, and Daniel could see Joe Smith's young, round face.

'Why, to Newtonstowe Prison, a'course, Mr Smith,' said the constable, with a note of embarrassment and regret in his voice.

At that, Samuel Smith raised his eyes briefly to the night sky. 'May God be my witness,' he said in a loud, clear voice, 'that no wrong has been done under my roof, not by me, nor any other.'

Then there was a confused babble of noise. A burly man, the enormously strong James Brown, pushed his way past Samuel, and went as if to raise his enormous fist at the policeman.

But Joe Smith pulled on the arm, just as his father cried out firmly, 'Peace, James! I'll not have any violence here, to spoil our cause!' And the muscular arm dropped feebly, as the man dropped his head in shame.

As Daniel still watched from his hiding place, the other two men also stepped out, both of them looking terrified. Then Samuel and Joe Smith, William Fletcher, James Brown and Harry Eades threw their shoulders back, and, with their heads held high, began the five-mile walk to the town of Newtonstowe – and to prison.

Chapter 11

TRIED AND TRANSPORTED

George stood by the kitchen range, leaning wearily against the wall. His head drooped. 'I should have been there with them,' he murmured.

But Annie went pink: 'No you should not!' she cried out. 'What would be the point of it?'

He looked up at her with dead eyes, whilst Daniel watched them, too tired now to speak. He had told what had happened; there was nothing left for him to say.

'Annie, you don't understand. None of you do,' said George. 'This night my friends and brothers are in prison, and I'm walking free. It isn't fair, and it isn't right.'

As long as Daniel could remember, Annie had never answered George back angrily, but she did now. 'Not fair! What kind of silly talk is that, George Wright? It's thanks to this poor lad here, who saved your life, and I'll always be grateful to him – always!'

With that she burst into angry tears, and strode past them into the scullery. They said nothing. The kitchen clock ticked. After about five minutes she came back, the marks of tears on her face. Then Mrs Brennan did something totally unexpected. She went across to the girl and put an arm around her shoulders, leading her to sit down at the kitchen table. 'There now, Annie, just you rest, and I'll fetch ye both a sup of ale,' she said, as Annie blinked up gratefully.

When she came back, Mrs Brennan stared into Daniel's exhausted face, streaked with blood and dirt. 'Have you a bed in your cottage for this lad, George?' she asked.

'Of course, Mrs Brennan,' George replied with surprise.

'Well, take him home with you tonight to rest. He's fair tired, and all for your sake, George. 'Tis right you should tend him.'

George's face was suddenly kind and soft. He reached out a hand to ruffle Daniel's hair, and his touch was clumsily tender. 'I know that, Mrs Brennan. And I'm not ungrateful to him, Annie. It's just that I'm thinking . . .' But he could not finish his sentence, which broke off into a husky cough.

Daniel remembered little after that, until he woke the next morning in bright, cold sunshine. George's cottage was tiny, with just one room and no upstairs floor. There was a simple, wooden bed in one corner, and one table and chair in the other, and that was all the furniture. But strings of onions hung from the ceiling with bunches of dried herbs, and the little house had a warm, clean smell, like that of the earth. Daniel lay in George's bed, with one eye open, watching as George crouched by the fire poking something in the black pot.

'I've made you some milk and water, lad,' he said at last, although he had not looked round, and Daniel could not imagine how he knew he was awake.

He brought the bowl across to the bed, and began to feed Daniel as though he were a baby. Daniel did not protest; his whole body ached, and there was something inexpressibly comforting about lying there as the warm milk trickled down his throat.

George's face was grave. Daniel knew what he was thinking, and asked, 'What will happen to them now, George? To Samuel and Joe?'

'I don't rightly know,' George sighed, 'but I'm going to see the Rector to ask if he can tell us. I reckon they'll be put on trial in Newtonstowe, and then . . . I don't know what.'

It was as if a cloud hung over the village, even though the sky was quite clear. The Winterstoke people stood around in groups, talking of the last night's events, then moved slowly about their business, shaking their heads. Two carriages arrived at the Manor, carrying important-looking men who drove away again after an hour, not looking to right or left. In the Rectory kitchen Mrs Brennan went about her cooking silently, without her usual stream of complaints and instructions. At one point Annie slammed down a plate with force, saying bitterly, 'The master, he don't seem able to look me in the eye today,' but Mrs Brennan did not protest.

Daniel went about all his tasks with a sick feeling in his

stomach, like hunger, but sharper. Once, carrying the full coal-scuttle through the hall to the Rector's study, he came face to face with Henry Forster, coming from the drawing-room, a book under his arm. 'Good day to you Master Henry,' he said, wondering if the other boy had heard. But the normally friendly face coloured pink, and Henry lowered his head, retreating into the room – as if he were ashamed of some bad thing he had done.

There was no sign of George after he left Daniel at the scullery door. It was dark before he appeared at last. Daniel rushed to him, clamouring to know what had happened. 'Did you see the master, did you, George? What did he say? Tell us, George.'

George held up a hand for silence, then slumped at the table. Slowly he told them how he had waited for the Reverend Forster on his usual morning walk, and asked what would happen to the Winterstoke men. The Rector had told him that they would be tried very soon, in just over a week's time. The fact that Samuel Smith had taken the warning notice from the tree was to be used against him; proving both that he had read it, and that he had no respect for it. 'The master do say he is sincerely sorry for what has happened,' George added grimly. 'So I asked him why he didn't keep his word to Samuel about the agreement.'

Annie put her head to her mouth. 'Oh George, you didn't! What did he say?'

'Hah, he said that he weren't going to be a party to sedition in this village, and that the labourers should learn to know their place. See, Dan'l? The gentlemen and the church and the magistrates always stick together.'

'What's sed . . . shun?' Daniel asked.

'Making trouble by standing up for your rights,' said George shortly. 'So anyway, I says to him then that if the masters couldn't afford to pay more, then they surely can't afford to keep their fine horses for hunting, and their carriages too. Then he advised me to mind my tongue, or else I'd find myself in as much trouble as my friends. So I left him then.'

Daniel closed his eyes and tried to imagine Joe Smith and his father in Newtonstowe prison, but he could not. They were strong countrymen, and belonged in the fields; the prison was a filthy, crowded place, with low-ceilinged cells, damp walls, and old straw infested with rats and mice. The terrible conditions were well-known for miles around, for every so often a man or boy from one of the villages would be sent there, often for a very small crime. Just a year ago a boy was whipped for stealing a loaf of bread, and his older brother, who stole with him, got two years in prison as well as the whipping. The magistrates were very harsh. It made Daniel tremble to think what they would do to the farm labourers who had ignored their warning.

'Yet, what have they done wrong?' he asked himself. 'It surely can't be a crime to gather in a room, and put bandages around your eyes, and say words? It *can't* be a crime!'

As the days dragged on, members of the men's families made the long walk to visit them, or else were lucky enough to hitch a lift with a carter. As soon as they returned, their stories spread like wildfire around the village: how the men were not allowed to talk to each other, how they were half-starved, how they already pined for the fields and the sky. Mary Smith leaned on George's arm in tears, as her two young sons clung to her skirt, their eyes wide with fear.

Daniel plucked up the courage to speak to her. 'Er, Mrs Smith, how . . . how's Joe taking it?'

She looked down at him, and the worried lines on her face softened for a moment. 'Why, it's young Dan'l. I'm grateful to you, my lad. If it weren't for you I wouldn't even have my own brother left to take care of me. And as for our Joe – he's fair enough. But he was given a beating for speaking out of turn, and I told him to watch his tongue. At least I was allowed to take him in a pie and a loaf, and the same for his father.'

At last the day of the trial came. Since the arrest the Rector had been acting very strangely, almost as if he were truly sorry for what had happened. Mrs Forster retired to her little sitting-room, and Dorothea was kept busy reading to her from the Bible. Henry and Frederick ran up to Daniel and whispered, 'Father says it's a bad business and we mustn't talk about it' – before turning away sadly.

The word in the village was that the Squire and the other farmers had drunk wine in celebration, but no one knew if it were true. At any rate, the Reverend Forster showed no such delight, and had surprised George the day before the trial by saying he could borrow the pony cart to take his sister and her children to Newtonstowe, together with anyone else they could fit in.

So it was that, very early in the morning, when it was still dark and frost sparkled on the ground, George took the reins, with Mary Smith, her two boys, Daniel, Mrs

Fletcher and Mrs Eades huddled under sacks behind him. Along the road they passed other people from Winterstoke, those who had set out even earlier on foot for the long walk to the courthouse.

They did not speak much on the journey. The women held hands, gazing at each other with serious faces, and Joe's two small brothers slept most of the way. When they reached the edge of the town, the sky was grey with golden streaks, and people were up and going to work. Occasionally a carter would wave to them, and call 'Good luck!' as if in full knowledge that these were Winterstoke folk, on their way to the now famous trial. For the 'Five men of Winterstoke' were already known for miles around.

'Why is that, George?' Daniel had asked the night before.

'It's because all the farm labourers in the land are waiting to see what happens. Though nothing's going to stop *them* making their own trade union, in any case, lad. And people are frightened of it.'

'What people?' asked Daniel.

'Important people. The government. The King. The men who own all the land, and think we're trying to take it away from them when all we're wanting is a decent wage to live on.'

Daniel was quiet, then. There were so many things he did not understand, but whilst a part of him wanted to ask questions, the other part wanted to run away from it all – back to the warm stove in the busy kitchen: the world that he knew.

The Newtonstowe Court House was an imposing building, with a fine clock on its gable. For those who were waiting for the trial of their loved ones, it seemed to tick the hours away cruelly. Already a small crowd waited in the market square in front, to be sure of seats in the public gallery. Two constables stood on the steps, their hands behind their backs, staring over the heads of the crowd.

Mary and the other two wives had hoped they might be allowed down into the grim cells below the building before the trial – just to wish their husbands good luck. But she came back from one of the duty constables shaking her head. It was not allowed. They would simply have to wave to the men across the crowded courtroom.

When at last the large, pale blue doors were opened the crowd surged forward. George held his sister's arm, and the two boys gripped his other hand. Daniel was left with Mrs Fletcher, who looked more tired and thin than ever, and Mrs Eades, who was a stout, red-faced woman, well able to support her friend. So Daniel followed them feeling rather left out, as if the drama that was about to happen had little to do with him, somehow. Yet it had. He knew it had, and felt guilty for his thought.

As they climbed the wide echoing stone staircase, and came out through a small door into the public gallery, George started to shoulder his way forward. 'Make way, we've relations here,' he murmured, and people parted sympathetically to let them through to the front row. They sat on the polished wooden bench, looking down on the huge panelled room with rows of seats for the jury, the witnesses and the lawyers. George pointed out to Daniel and his nephews the bench for the judge and the raised dock where the prisoners would stand. The room was lit by the pale morning sun shining through tall windows with curved tops.

Daniel watched open-mouthed as the lawyers filed in and the judge took his place. He kept whispering, 'Who's that? And who's that?' to George, who laid a stern finger to his lips and shook his head. He pointed, and Daniel saw why. The prisoners were being brought up the steps into the docks, and as they appeared a strange sigh rustled round the public gallery – a sound of astonishment and of grief. Daniel stared at the shorn heads and pale faces of the five men in their grey prison clothes. But the three women beside him showed no sign of shock. They straightened their backs in pride, and Mary Smith raised one hand in greeting to her husband and son. The men glanced up briefly, then back at the Judge.

'Samuel Smith, Joseph Smith, William Fletcher, James Brown and Harold Eades of the parish of Winterstoke in the County of Somerset, I hereby charge you that on the nineteenth day of November in the year of our Lord eighteen hundred and thirty-five, you did unlawfully administer an oath to one Thomas Leggat also of the aforesaid parish of Winterstoke in the County of Somerset, which said oath was also taken by all of you here present, against the dignity and peace of our Lord, the King and his Crown . . .'

So it began, and it was as if a torrent of incomprehensible words battered Daniel's brain. The light poured through the tall windows, the men in the dock gripped the polished brass rail with their hands, and speech after speech was made. Samuel Smith was speaking for all five men; he stood with his head held high, and answered all the questions with a firm, clear voice.

'And did you not entice your fellow labourers into a meeting with illegal representatives of the Agricultural Members' Friendly Society?' asked the prosecution with a sneer.

'No, sir, I did not,' replied Samuel, again and again.

There was a slight pause, as the Judge consulted some papers, so Daniel took the chance to whisper to George, 'Samuel's so clever, George. They'll not send him to prison, not never!'

George shook his head. 'Him being clever or not don't make no difference, Dan'l. See the judge there? He's the cousin of the Prime Minister himself. See the Grand Jury? Why, you'll recognize Mr Plumptree the Magistrate, our Squire's brother, and Mr Eliot, his cousin, who's a Magistrate too. As for the other ten, lad, they're all farmers hereabouts. I tell you, there's no chance of justice in this room!'

Mary hushed him. The first witness was being called – and Thomas Leggat went up into the witness box, looking smart in a new suit of clothes. Daniel thought they must be paid for with the money the Squire had handed him. Then he thought back to the night when Leggat gripped him in the darkness, and shuddered.

Thomas Leggat's thin face was scarlet, and he carefully did not look at his fellow labourers. But Harry Eades glared at him, and raised a fist, and Joe shouted 'Shame!' At that Samuel Smith raised a hand in warning, and they both hung their heads. William Fletcher looked tired and beaten; James Brown stood as if in a dream.

Daniel was amazed at the mess Leggat made of what he had to say. He mumbled and asked for questions to be repeated, and answered 'I don't know, sir' to so many questions that Daniel was astonished they did not throw him out of the courtroom there and then. He said he could not remember exactly what had happened at Samuel Smith's house, nor who had been there. When he was asked if it had been the men he saw in the dock, he hung his head and whispered, 'I think so, sir,' so that the Judge told him sharply to speak up.

'He's sorry for what he's done,' Daniel thought with a great surge of hope, 'and so he's trying to undo it. They can't possibly send them to prison now.'

Yet when the time came for the Judge to sum up he turned to the Jury with a severe look on his face.

'You have heard, gentlemen, from the witness Thomas Leggat, a clear and damning account of the events of the night in question, when this evil oath was taken. It will prove to you beyond any doubt that the accused men were determined on their plot to bend their innocent fellow labourers to their wicked purpose . . .'

'But Leggat didn't,' Daniel began to whisper.

'Hush, child,' hissed Mary Smith, not taking her eyes off the Judge in his splendid robe and white wig.

He was turning to the prisoners, with a look of contempt on his face. 'Have you anything to say before the Grand Jury considers its verdict?' he asked.

Samuel Smith raised a hand. 'Might I hand you something I have written?' he asked respectfully. The Judge nodded, and the piece of paper was passed across to him. For a few minutes he said nothing, simply read what was written with a look of deep dislike on his face. Then he raised his head and read the words in a fast mumble, not looking at the Jury at all, but into the air. In any case, the members of the Jury were fiddling with their canes or boots, and were not listening. But Daniel and George heard every word, and Mary Smith reached across and joined hands with Mrs Fletcher and Mrs Eades.

Samuel Smith's message to the court was simple. It said: 'My Lord, if we have broken any law, we did not mean to do so. We have hurt no man, nor his property. We were uniting together to save ourselves, our wives and children from utter misery and starvation, and that was our sole aim. We acted according to our belief in what is right, and our faith in the teachings of Jesus Christ our Lord, Amen.'

The Jury took no longer than twenty minutes to consider the verdict. They returned with grim faces, and Mr Plumptree stood.

'Guilty,' he said. Daniel felt Mary Smith grow stiff with fear, and the two boys began to cry – only to be silenced by a stern look from their mother.

'Now don't you make your father ashamed of you,' she whispered. 'You be as brave as your brother down there!'

So the two little boys just clung to each other, as Mrs Fletcher and Mrs Eades began to murmur a prayer, and George held his sister's hand.

The Judge was about to speak again. All the people in the public gallery sat like statues, and Daniel held his breath. So great was the silence in that room that he fancied he could hear the dust falling all around him, and time stop. Time . . . what did it mean? When one second could stretch out so cruelly, as it now did?

Looking sternly at the five prisoners, the Judge coughed. 'I feel I have no choice in this matter, but I must pronounce on you the sentence which the Act of Parliament has imposed. It is to act as a warning to other men, who may also be tempted to break the law of this land, and threaten the security of King and Country. Therefore I judge that each of you shall be taken from this place, and transported across the seas to Australia, or whatever such place His Majesty sees fit, for the term of seven years.'

Immediately, Samuel Smith put an arm around the shoulders of his son, who was staring up to where his mother sat. The boy's face was pale, and he could not stem the cry of horror that rose to his lips. Mary Smith leaned on George and looked as if she were about to faint, whilst Mrs Fletcher and Mrs Eades threw their aprons over their faces and began to weep. Some men at the back of the public gallery cried out 'For shame! For shame!' but were silenced when a burly constable appeared behind them.

Daniel did not want to believe what he heard. Only the night before he had sat in the kitchen with Annie and George, listening with fascinated horror as George told them of the dreaded convict ships which carry men to work as slave labour in Australia.

'Men die like flies in them ships,' George had said. 'They do die from beatings, from sickness, from hunger. And sometimes because the hearts in them have broken.'

Annie had drawn in her breath sharply: 'But George, that's a punishment for real criminals! For thieves and murderers! They'd never do it to your men!'

George had simply shaken his head, looking at her with dread in his eyes.

And now it was over, Daniel remembered Annie's words and cried out, 'They can't do it to them! It's wicked!' – his voice lost in the general noise.

Nobody in his group said anything to him. But a stranger sitting behind – a man in a farm labourer's smock like George – heard him and nodded his head with grim slowness. 'Oh yes, they can, my lad. They can do what they like. But you mark my words – these men'll be remembered for ever. Your own great-grandchildren will know about the Winterstoke Five, and how they was punished!'

Chapter 12

GEORGE'S PROMISE

It was as if Winterstoke were sleeping. People kept inside their houses, only going out if they had to. Then they walked slowly, with bent shoulders, as if a great weight had been placed on their necks. Squire Plumptree was never seen; when at last it was Sunday and people looked for him in church he arrived late for the service, and strode to his pew with his head in the air, not looking to right or to left. His family followed, with embarrassed and anxious expressions on their faces, or so some of the old women said. Daniel thought they looked just the same. The Rector preached a long sermon about forgiveness, but Daniel was not sure who was supposed to forgive whom.

Nobody could forgive Thomas Leggat, which is why it was lucky for him that he was never seen again in the village. He disappeared after the trial, and his new wife – a maid at the Manor House – left their ramshackle cottage on the Squire's estate and vanished.

'She must have arranged to meet him somewhere,' Annie said. 'But I'd pity a woman who could love as wicked a man as that.'

'Oh, he had his thirty pieces of silver, like Judas,' said George bitterly. 'But don't waste thoughts on him, Annie. Think of Susan Fletcher and her little ones, turned off the land by Mr Winterton. That's wickedness! Luckily for her she could go to her father, just seven miles off.'

'What . . . what about the baby?' Daniel asked in a small voice.

'Bad. Worse than ever now. It's not likely to live, I reckon – or that's what all the women do say,' Annie replied sadly.

The little community felt stunned, still reeling from the shock waves of that terrible day at court. George wore a permanent look of rage mixed with suffering, which made Annie whisper to Mrs Brennan, 'Makes you afraid he'll do something desperate, like. Try to rescue them, or something . . .'

But there was no chance of that. The five Winterstoke men had been taken to the Hulks, the dreaded prison ships at Portsmouth. These were old wooden warships which, when their fighting days were over, were used as floating gaols. The toughest and most violent criminals were put there, because it was so hard to escape from the Hulks. After all, what chance was there of swimming, with the heavy manacles and chains which shackled the men's legs, so that they could only walk with a slow shuffle? Out of every three men who went to the Hulks one always died, because of the bad food, the cold, the cruelty of the guards and the lack of doctors. Even the most simple country boy had heard of the terrible Hulks. It was said that men were actually *glad* to be transported after waiting there, because anything seemed better.

'Why did they have to go on those ships? They're not real criminals,' Daniel asked Annie. She shook her head helplessly but said nothing.

'Will they really stay in Australia for seven years? Will they, Annie?'

She sighed. 'Oh, your questions, Dan'l. Of course they'll stay for the full time, if they live that long. But lots of men die. They do say it's terrible hard in Australia.'

'But *why* send them all that way? They haven't killed anyone or done any real crime. So *why*, Annie?'

Just then Daniel heard a soft step behind him, and felt a hand on his shoulder, as Annie looked up with a sad smile. 'Oh George, you answer the boy,' she said.

George looked down at Daniel. 'Annie can't answer your questions, my lad, because there aren't any answers. Not ones any Christian would understand.'

'But I want to *understand*, George!' Daniel was desperate.

George sat down at the kitchen table and pulled Daniel towards him with both hands, so that the boy stood right in front of him and their faces were on the same level. 'Listen here,' he said seriously, 'you can ask me anything you like, but what I'm saying is that some things are beyond understanding. Any answer I'll give you will be as hard for you to believe, as if I said that the Devil himself came with eyes like fire and decided those men should be punished! I heard you say that Samuel an' Joe an' the rest did nothing wrong. Well, you're right! But you see, lad, the government is frightened of 'em.'

'What? The King and them?' Daniel asked, in a disbelieving voice.

'Aye, the very same. They're afraid of what the Winterstoke men stand for – just working men like me saying they'll join together to ask for a decent wage, that's all. It's never happened in this country but it's happening now, all over. The King, the Prime Minister and all those great men – they're as frightened as you'd be if you walked out of here and met a lion in the lane. The fact is this, Dan: our men have been sent to Australia as an example to others, that's all. The King, he's saying, "Don't do like they did or you'll be punished too." But it won't work.'

For a few minutes Daniel said nothing, thinking about what George had said. The only sound in the room was the brisk rub of Annie's cloth as she polished the brass candlesticks, and of course the steady ticking of the great kitchen clock. As Daniel glanced up at the clock face he felt a curious shivery sensation, as if he had forgotten something again, something he would be in trouble for not remembering, something to do with the clock . . . the passing of time . . .

'What is it, Dan'l? Stop worrying, laddie!' whispered Annie, reaching out her hand to pat his arm.

'Oh, it's all right. I was just thinking about it all. George, how old will Joe be when they get back?'

George looked bitter, as if he could hardly bear the question. 'He'll be twenty-two, and all his boyhood gone. If he gets back at all. And if he does – *when* he does – I hope he'll come back to this country and carry on fighting for what's right. And I hope he'll make them that sent him away live to be sorry for the day they did it!'

'Oh George,' Annie said softly, 'you didn't ought to preach hatred. Not to the boy.'

At that George glared at her, clenching his fist into a huge ball, and staring down at it. 'And why not?' he shouted, without looking up, 'when hatred is just what I feel? Don't be preaching all that nonsense about forgiveness to me, woman, because I'll never forgive them that betrayed my brother-in-law and my nephew – never! Don't don't ask me to, you hear me?'

With that he lurched to his feet, and strode from the room, banging the scullery door behind him. Daniel and Annie stared at each other with white, shocked faces. There was nothing to say; George's anger made them both feel ashamed, somehow, as though they had let him down. But neither of them understood why.

Next morning Daniel was still asleep on his bed in front of the stove, when he felt something shaking him. He snuggled down still further, and the shakes grew more fierce. 'Wake up, wake up!' hissed Annie.

'Mmmmh . . . what is it?' he mumbled, deep in a dream about a delicious golden chicken pie, baked especially for him and with no one else to share it. He did not want to wake up.

'George is at the scullery door, wantin' to be speaking with you, Dan,' Annie whispered. 'He looks fair strange this morning, Dan. Go and see what's wrong. And don't worry, 'tis a full hour before Mrs Brennan do start.'

George was standing in the cold darkness, a piece of sacking wrapped around his shoulders on top of his thick smock, to keep out the chill dawn wind. In the light from his flickering lantern Daniel could see a strange, wild expression on his face, as if he would burst from keeping all his thoughts inside him a moment longer.

'I . . . I want to ask you summat, Dan, summat important. I've a lot on my mind, lad, and I want to know your feelings before I go about my day's work. So I can plan, like . . .'

He sounded hesitant, not like the old George at all. Daniel stared at him. 'What *is* it, George?' he asked.

'Well, Dan'l, it's hard to put . . . but what I want to know is – will you throw in your lot with me, Dan?'

'Why, I don't know what you mean, George.'

'Will you come away with me?'

'*Away* with you?' Daniel repeated, knowing he sounded foolish.

George made an impatient movement with his hand. 'I mean to say, if I was to ask you to travel with me, would you do it?'

'Not to Australia, George!' Daniel cried out. He was not very sure exactly where Australia was, but he thought about the place so often since the sentence of transportation was passed that it grew more and more terrible in his mind – a dreadful place, full of monsters and danger.

'No, Dan'l, not to Australia.'

'Then where?'

'Wherever we have to go to take the message.'

'What message? I don't understand you. You mean leave Winterstoke altogether? You mean . . .' Daniel blurted, but George held up a warning hand and glanced over Daniel's shoulder.

'Look, not a word to Annie, mind. I want you to think about coming away with me, lad, that's all I'll say now – to give you summat to be turning over in your mind. I'm off to Mary's now, that's why I'm up so early. I do believe that it's today they're taken off the Hulks and put on the boat for Australia. So I must see Mary and pray with her a while. I'll come back and talk to you later, about when Mrs Brennan has gone to Winterton's dairy.' Saying that, he turned and walked off into the lightening dawn.

It was several hours before he returned, timing it perfectly as he had promised. The breakfast had been prepared and cleared away, and Mrs Brennan had left a huge pot of delicious stew simmering on the stove, for the family's lunch. Green vegetables lay chopped, ready for cooking later, and Daniel had peeled all the potatoes for the meal, piling them with salt and water in the black iron pan.

Mrs Brennan had gone to choose her cheeses, as she did not trust anyone else to make such an important decision, so Annie and Daniel could snatch the time to sit down for a rest – before the cook returned with her constant stream of orders. George found them sitting at the end of the table nearest the splendidly hot stove – Annie sewing a collar, and Daniel whittling at a piece of wood with a kitchen knife.

George stood for a second, looking down at them but saying nothing. His face was such a mixture of sadness and anger that Daniel caught his breath. 'It's happened. They sailed this morning,' George muttered in a husky voice, then flopped down and buried his face in his hands.

At last he looked up again, and fumbled in his pocket, drawing out a piece of paper. 'Samuel and Joe wrote to Mary a day or two ago,' he said, 'and she let me bring the letter to show you.' He held it out, then remembered that neither Daniel nor Annie could read. So he drew the letter back to himself, and held it up with hands that trembled slightly, reading in the same low husky voice.

'Thank you, my dear wife, Mary, for all your love and kindness to me, and as long as I live I will try to repay your loyalty. As soon as we reach the place they have sent us I shall try to write to you, if paper and pen be available to prisoners such as I. Let us never forget the vows we made to each other before God at the altar, and though we shall be apart for a while, I shall always think of you with love, as though I were in your presence. Do not worry about me, my dear Mary. We shall work together for good, and I know that by the grace of God we shall see the day when we are together again. Look after my little sons David and Jonathan for me, and always tell them that their father did no harm. May the Lord bless you and look after you all, and show His mercy to you. Your loving husband, Samuel.'

Tears filled Annie's eyes. Daniel looked down, not knowing what to say. 'And Joe's written a note on the end here,' George said in a quiet voice. 'Listen an' I'll read that, too.' He cleared his throat:

'My dear mother, I send to you my loving greetings and hope you are well, as I am. Sometimes I am afraid of what shall befall me, but my father is good and gives me strength. In case anything happens to me, I want you to give my knife as I made at the forge to Daniel Richards of the Rectory, as I cannot share it between my two brothers and they are so young they might cut themselves. Mother, I will always act as you have taught me, and try to do right in all things. Please believe that my father and I will come back to you, my dear mother, with love from your son, Joseph.'

There was silence when George finished. Then he dug deeply into his pocket again and pulled out the knife Joe had shown Daniel that evening – which seemed so long ago now. For a few minutes Daniel could not touch it, but simply stared at it where it lay on the table. Then he picked it up gently, and cradled it in his two hands, whispering, 'I never had anything so fine before – not of my *own*, George.'

''Tis a pity you have to get it at such a cost,' replied George in a hard voice.

Daniel put down the knife as if it were red hot, and stared down at it with quick tears in his eyes. 'I'd rather not have it at all, and have Joe back!' he retorted.

George said nothing. He was not listening, but seemed to be concentrating on something else, his face grave with an abstracted expression. At last he took a deep breath, as though he had made up his mind about something. 'Oh, I know . . . but never mind about the knife now. I want to say something properly, like, and I want you two to be my witnesses.'

Annie put her hand to her mouth in alarm. 'No more of them oaths what's against the law, George! What do you want to promise?'

'I've made a decision, Annie. I'm making a vow that the story of the Winterstoke men is known in every village in this country. I won't let them be forgotten! I want to be sure that there isn't a labourer in this land who doesn't know what they did, and how they were rewarded for it!'

'How will you do that, George?' asked Daniel.

'I'm going on my way,' George replied. Annie drew in her breath with a sharp gasp.

'Going where?' she asked in a small voice.

George reached across and enclosed her hand, reddened from hard work, in his huge brown fist. 'I'm sorry, Annie, but I'm leaving Winterstoke, and I'm taking to the roads, and I shall go where God takes me. Look, I can't stay here, listening to the Rector preaching his cant in church of a Sunday, remembering how he went back on his word. I can't walk in this village, and see the Squire ride past me, and his lady all in silk and fur – knowing what he did, and that all the while our men are being beaten near to death in a prison camp in Australia. I can't stand it. So I'm going away. The way I see it, I was spared their fate for a *purpose*, Annie, not just to go on tilling the Rector's land. So I'm first going to walk to Yorkshire –'

'Walk? To Yorkshire?' cried Daniel, to whom Yorkshire seemed almost as far away as Australia.

'Aye. And on the way I'm going to talk to every man I meet. I'm going to find the men who organize these trade unions, and speak at their meetings. And I'm going to preach in the open like Samuel and the other Methodists – only the message I'll be taking to them is about much more than Methodism!'

'Oh-h, they'll arrest you, George!' wailed Annie.

'That may be. But I have to do as I believe. And I want you to come with me, Dan'l.'

'Me?' Daniel was shocked.

'Aye, lad. I've talked about this with Mary, and she said she can spare me. I'll be doing what jobs I can to send her money, but in any case, she's moving into Newtonstowe to be near all Samuel's cousins, who'll take care of her and the children. You've no family, lad. Mary said that if you threw in your lot with me, we could be like family to each other. It's a lonely path for me.' His face softened as he said this, and looked from Daniel to Annie.

'But what – what about me, George?' whispered Annie, with a tiny note of panic in her voice.

He gripped her hand more firmly. 'You'll find someone else to take care of you, Annie. You're a sweet, pretty girl and you'll make some lucky man a good wife. You've no shortage of admirers in these parts; there was plenty of men right jealous when I started walking out with you! But you can't share in what I have to do. I can't think of my happiness as a man. I have to think of what I owe to Samuel, Joe, and the others.'

'So we won't be wed, George?' Her face was afraid.

'We won't wed, Annie, I'm sorry,' he replied, in the gentlest tone Daniel had ever heard him use. For a long time Annie stared at him with a look of utter astonishment on her face. Then she burst into tears and ran from the room.

Daniel and George were left looking at each other as if they had seen each other for the first time.

'Well, lad,' said George, biting his lip.

'When . . . ?'

'At the end of the week. I'll tell the Reverend tomorrow. Will you come with me, Dan'l?'

Daniel was surprised to see how eager George looked. It was the first time he had ever seen the tall strong man as someone who . . . who *needed* something, and something which he, Daniel, could actually give. Yet words would not come. He gazed around the kitchen, then rose and walked to the stove, leaning against it until it grew too hot and he had to move away. To leave all this for the cold, unknown roads – perhaps for danger . . . The thought horrified him.

George must have seen it in his face, for he looked down, clearly disappointed. 'I thought you'd say yes right away, Dan. You said to me you wanted to do whatever I do.'

'Oh, I will! I'm sure I will. But I can say for certain tomorrow, George? When you come and tell the Reverend? Can I just wait a while to think . . . er . . . what I'd say to him myself? So's he won't think me ungrateful, George!' Daniel knew that he was pleading for time to think, and he knew that George knew it too.

'All right, laddie,' said George, rising wearily to his feet. 'I know it's a hard life I'm offering you, but at least you'll be a free man, and not just a servant here. We've got important things to do, Dan. I know you'll come with me, if you think – like I do – that it's the right thing to do.'

All day Daniel thought. He felt like someone sitting on the edge of a cliff, dangling his legs and staring into the dizzy emptiness of the air, whilst all the time a dreadful creature drew closer and closer behind him, ready to push . . . What should he do? It was so hard, so very hard to make up his mind. He knew that for George there would be no problem – only one way was clear. The knife, which he had tied around his waist with a piece of string, banged against him under his smock, accusingly. Once he held it in one hand, very tightly, and whispered, 'I'm *not* afraid. I *will* go with George, Joe. I will tell your story to those that'll listen. Only . . .' And he looked around the kitchen once more – warm and familiar. Everything in it conspired to keep him there; it was as if the very pots and pans set up a rattling inside his head to drown George's words.

Mrs Brennan was in a bad mood all day, for a pudding had burnt inside the oven spilling boiling syrup everywhere, and, to make matters worse, the stew had boiled over and caked the surface of the stove. Though it had not been Daniel's fault (for he was sweeping the bakery as she had ordered, whilst she, taking gingerbread men to Miss Dorothea, had forgotten her meal) Mrs Brennan had boxed his ears and snapped that he must look to his work.

So, when the family had eaten their evening meal and all the washing-up was finished, Mrs Brennan and Annie disappeared, leaving Daniel to his task. He opened the main oven door. There was a smell of burnt sugar from inside, and the warmth hit him full in the face – even though they had let the stove go out for the cleaning.

He knelt, and peered into the blackness of the oven, his bucket of water ready beside him. But he did not start work right away. Instead, he sat back on his heels and thought of all that George had said. He tried to picture Samuel and Joe Smith, and William Fletcher, Harry Eades and James Brown on that crowded ship, tossing on the sea, travelling far from Winterstoke. He thought of George, his best friend, leaving to wander round the country, perhaps to be beaten and arrested, perhaps to freeze under some strange hedgerow.

Suddenly he was aware of water trickling down his cheek. He touched himself with one dirty finger, to find that his face was wet with tears. So Daniel allowed himself to lean forward on the stove, and cry at last – pouring out all his sadness at what had happened, his confusion at the reasons for it, his fear of the future – all welling up in his eyes and pouring down his cheeks, and dropping in great wet patches on the dull black metal of the stove. Without thinking what he was doing, Daniel rubbed his own tears into the stove, spreading the wetness in wider and wider circles, until the iron was bright . . .

But inside the open door it was burnt and black. The oven's interior was dark and dirty, like a mysterious cave. 'If only I could escape,' Daniel thought. 'If only I could grow very small and climb inside the stove, and curl up into a ball, so that George could not possibly find me, and I wouldn't have to make up my mind. Shall I go with him? Or shall I stay? I *must* go! But there isn't much time to decide . . .'

The clock still ticked on the kitchen wall, but as Daniel wearily dipped his old cloth into the warm water and leaned forward to tackle the oven, that comforting regular sound seemed to cease. There was silence in the kitchen, and silence in his own mind – where those dizzy questions had revolved again and again. Silence and peace, as he rubbed and rubbed . . . And then the blackness seemed to rush forward to meet him, and he was falling, falling into its empty wastes.

Chapter 13

IN THE CHURCHYARD

I don't know what to do . . . to do . . .

'Daniel! Daniel!'

There's nothing I can do. Oh George . . .

'Daniel!'

Daniel heard the voice calling him, deep in the back of his mind, buried, but pushing its way forward to the light. As it grew closer it brought with it all he had forgotten, as if particles of memory, flying everywhere, suddenly started to take shape.

'Dan! Come on, what are you doing?'

'Just look at him, Evie!'

'Like a puppy on a rug!' There was laughter near his ear, a sound full of affection, which Daniel recognized. Then somebody tickled him, and he jack-knifed his body to avoid it. It was hard beneath him, and he could not understand why. Then he opened his eyes, and realized.

He was curled up on the floor, in front of the old stove, in the dust left by the builders. He could feel it in his hair, and smell it in his nostrils – the fine dust of years and years. It made him shudder.

'Darling, you're cold! Come on, get up now and we'll take you up to bed. You can't sleep curled up like a little dog on the floor!'

That voice. A loving voice: a mother's voice. His own mother's voice. And over him, as he opened his eyes wide now, were bending the two faces he loved best in all the world. But Daniel Richards had no parents. For a moment he felt miserable and confused; the feeling of relief mingled with a powerful sense of loss.

'You must have dropped off, Dan.' His father was heaving him to his feet, taking all the weight of Daniel's floppy, aching body. More than just stiff, Daniel felt as if he had been kicked about a rugby field, and his head ached.

'Not . . . asleep,' he said slowly.

His mother looked anxious suddenly. 'What's wrong, Dan? You look a bit . . . strange. Did you have a bad dream, or something?'

'Not a dream,' Daniel replied in the same slow, weary voice. Then he repeated the words, this time with a questioning note in his voice: 'Not a dream?'

He allowed himself to be led upstairs like a baby, or a sleepwalker whom people are afraid to waken unless they give the sleeper a sudden shock. And indeed, shock was what he felt – his memories of George and Annie were as vivid as ever, but now they walked side by side with the reality of his parents. This life. Now.

As he struggled into his pyjamas, one thought was uppermost in his mind – the fear that he would forget all *that* in just a matter of hours, as he had forgotten *this*. And he did not want to forget; he knew it was important that he should not forget.

He was lying in the darkness, thinking, when his father came in. 'Just thought I'd check you're OK,' he murmured, bending to kiss Daniel's forehead.

'Why shouldn't I be?' asked Daniel.

'Oh, I don't know. But you looked so pale and shocked downstairs that I felt a bit worried. It was as if you'd seen a ghost.'

'Dad?'

'Yes?'

'Are there such things? In old houses like this one?'

'Oh no, I don't think so. Why?'

Daniel was silent for a minute, afraid his father could not possibly believe him, and so might laugh . . . That would be terrible. He could not bear anyone to laugh. Then he blurted, 'But mightn't there be people, people who'd lived here before . . . still here? In some way? I don't mean in a frightening way. I just mean that they might want . . . want to tell us what happened to them all, years and years ago.'

'I don't really see how they could, Danny,' said Dr Richards gently. 'But then if you're a doctor like me, or a scientist, you tend to believe in things you can see. Things you can prove. I've never had to examine a sick ghost!'

'Oh, of course you haven't, Dad!' There was a note of real irritation and disappointment in Daniel's voice, which his father heard.

'I'm sorry, son. I know you've had a strange dream, or something – I can tell. But you can't expect me to share it, because it wasn't my dream, was it? Just forget about it now, and go to sleep.'

'*Not* a dream,' murmured Daniel, as his father went out, leaving the door ajar so that the light from the landing filtered comfortingly into the room.

When he woke to the bright morning light, he tried out those words again – this time with a bright, confident ring. 'It jolly well wasn't a dream, I know it,' he said aloud, looking at his room crammed with the familiar books and toys. He thought wonderingly of the children in the cottages, with nothing to play with, working like adults even when they were nine or ten, and he shook his head. It seemed important to cling to his conviction that all that was not a dream – otherwise he would be betraying what he knew, what *was*, just as Thomas Leggat had betrayed the men of Winterstoke.

He went downstairs. The messy kitchen was full of sunlight, and the builders had already arrived. Evie Richards was making tea and chatting to them about her plans.

'Well, are you taking this old thing out then, missus?' asked the older man, jerking one thumb over his shoulder in the direction of the *Herald Patent* stove.

Daniel's mother folded her arms, her head on one side, and sighed. 'I really can't decide. But in the meantime, you can be seeing to the sink unit and the cupboards along this side. Don't worry, I'll make up my mind about the wretched thing today!'

Daniel walked slowly across the room and stood by the stove, resting his palm for a second on its flat top. The voices in the room seemed to fade away as he looked, so that the memory of all that he had experienced was all the more powerful. And nothing surprised him any more. He understood quite clearly how the hard work and the tears of that boy who had lived a hundred and fifty years ago had so impregnated this old stove that his spirit had once again been released for Daniel to join. That was all. It had really happened.

Yet Daniel felt an aching disappointment, as if someone had suddenly snatched away a book he was enjoying, so that he would never be able to discover the end of the story. He wanted to know what happened to George. Perhaps he changed his mind and married Annie; perhaps he was arrested in the end and punished. Did the five transported men live to return to their families in Winterstoke? And what of Daniel Richards – did he find the courage to go with George? 'Oh, I hope he did,' Daniel thought. But he would never know. For history, he thought angrily, is always the stories of kings and queens and prime ministers and battles fought and won. 'We never learn about the ordinary people. Nobody knows *their* history,' he whispered, feeling the rusty iron, quite cold to his touch.

Not long afterwards Mrs Richards held out Daniel's jacket. She already wore her own. 'Come on, lazybones, it's a lovely day. Let's go for a walk to keep out of the builders' way.'

'Oh, all right. But where shall we go?' said Daniel reluctantly. He hated long walks.

'Not far, though a good long walk would do you good! I thought we'd go and study the church – properly, I mean. They sell a little booklet inside which gives its history. We should learn about the place we live in, don't you think?'

'I suppose so,' Daniel sighed.

But he was glad to get out of the house for a while, because it oppressed him. So different now, with white painted wood instead of the thick, dark brown varnish which used to cover everything, and yet the same place, with the same walls, which had watched silently over the lives that were lived within them. 'If walls could talk . . .' people said. But perhaps they could; now Daniel believed anything to be possible.

The sun shone on spring flowers in the hedgerows, and gleamed on the dew. Everything seemed new and fresh, and Daniel breathed deeply, to banish forever that dead smell of dust. Almost as if she could read his mind, his mother said, 'Gosh, it's good to get away from all that building mess, isn't it? The dust gets everywhere! Hey, Dan, isn't this country air marvellous? Not a bit like London!'

'Mmmmm,' grunted Daniel. He was thinking how odd it was that people could think the same thing at the same minute – and so why should it not happen across time? What if there had been a boy, in a certain house, with the same name as another boy who came much later? After all, it was not such an unusual name. So why should there not be . . . contact, between them?

Yet the sunlight and the fresh air made it all seem

unlikely. 'Too much of a coincidence,' Daniel thought, as he wandered along at his mother's side, down the hill towards the church. 'Maybe they were right, after all, and it was just a peculiar dream that seemed realistic. Dreams usually do . . . and in dreams time goes all funny. I must have only been asleep a few minutes, dreaming of weeks and weeks. I think it must . . .' He furrowed his brow; already he was losing his faith.

But there before them was the churchyard, with the drystone wall still dividing it from the rolling farmland on the other side. His heart thumped, so vivid was his recollection of running in fear like a hunted animal, climbing the wall, and landing on . . . yes, that ancient flat stone slab was still there.

'Let's go inside the church,' said his mother as they walked under the lych gate and along the path.

'No,' said Daniel, with sudden determination, 'let's just explore the churchyard first, then do the church. I don't want to go inside just yet.'

Winterstoke churchyard was very large, stretching in humps and bumps around the pretty Norman church, accommodating itself to the hilly lie of the land. There were rows of newish graves at the top – white marble oblongs filled with green glass chippings like gravel, and decorated with flowers in vases – some of them clearly plastic. Then, nearer the church there were the old graves – mossy tombstones weathered to soft and mellow shades of grey and gold, some of them carved in the shapes of angels or books or urns, some plain flat standing stones, with beautifully cut lettering overgrown with lichen and moss.

Daniel and his mother wandered in different directions. Occasionally she would call out as she noticed a particularly good carving, exclaiming once, 'Oh, I must bring my sketchbook down here. It's wonderful!' Daniel just nodded quietly. He felt peaceful, and somehow at home.

Eve Richards was bending over, about a hundred yards away, talking over her shoulder to him, not expecting any reply. She was idly pulling at the brambles which covered a small, plain sloping gravestone near the wall of the church. 'Gosh, some of these things are covered up,' she called. 'It makes them look so neglected. A bit sad, really . . .'

Daniel stood looking at the sky. 'Yes,' he said absent-mindedly, 'it makes you wonder who they all were.'

'Hey!' Suddenly his mother's hand started to work furiously, and she used her feet too – scraping at the tangled undergrowth around a gravestone. 'Hey, Dan – come over here. You'll never guess!'

'Guess what?'

But she was too busy tugging at the brambles, throwing chunks of moss to one side, picking up a sharp stone to scratch and scrape. 'Come on, Dan!' she called, with such a great excitement in her voice that Dan felt a thrill – a tremor deep inside him, as if he knew its cause.

'What is it, Mum?'

With an urgency he did not fully understand he started towards her, jumping over anonymous green mounds and skirting leaning crosses. When he arrived at his mother's side she was staring down with an expression of utter disbelief and amazement on her face. 'Well – isn't that the most peculiar, extraordinary thing? I simply can't believe it.'

'*Look!*' she almost shouted, pointing down at the grave-stone. 'Can you manage to read it? It's rather difficult because the letters are so worn – but listen, Dan!' And, pausing every now and then to be sure of a word, she read aloud the old, worn lettering on the little stone:

In Memory of
DANIEL RICHARDS
died April 30th 1894
in the seventieth year of his age
A true and faithful servant
to the Reverend John Forster
of this parish,
and to his son
the Reverend Henry Forster
who erected this stone.
Rest in Peace

Eve Richards folded her arms thoughtfully. 'Well, I must say I've never known a coincidence like that. Exactly the same name, Dan! And he must have lived in the Rectory – our house! You wouldn't believe it, would you? Just wait until we tell Dad.'

Daniel could not speak. He nodded, staring down at the words, and it was as if a voice in his head – his own voice – was speaking aloud in an echoing hall in a nameless land that was outside time: 'So that's it. You didn't go with George, you didn't go anywhere, Daniel. You stayed in that kitchen until you died, blackleading the stove, doing jobs for the family, knowing your place in the world – even when Henry grew up and became Rector in his father's place. A good and faithful servant, Daniel. You didn't have the courage to leave . . . But I don't blame you. I don't blame you at all, do you hear me?'

Like a tinkling, fragile note of wind chimes, there seemed to come drifting into his mind the echo of a voice. Sadly, far away, it whispered, 'There was nothing I could do . . . Nothing I could do . . .'

Perhaps that was true, after all, Daniel thought. Yet *both* things were true: George Wright's belief that you had to strike out and simply *try*, at whatever the cost, and Daniel's doubts. You could not prove who was right, not even if you had all the evidence in front of you. For who is to know if things change through individual men, or through great waves, great patterns in history? Daniel shook his head, conscious only of an enormous pity for Daniel, for George, for Annie, for all of them who did their best, however poor. And who were long, long dead.

'What are you thinking?' asked his mother.

'Oh nothing . . . I mean, I was wondering about this person.'

The sun was really warm now, and its golden light made the little neglected stone look mellow, as if it was glad to be found. Daniel turned quickly to his mother with shining eyes. 'I'm going to come back this afternoon and tidy it up properly. I'll put some flowers on it!' he said.

'That's a nice thought. For the sake of the name.' She smiled, resting an arm on his shoulders.

'Mum – how do you find out the history of a place? A village like this? I'm thinking I'd like to do a sort of . . . a project on Winterstoke.'

'That's a terrific idea. We could help! I could do some drawings for you, and Dad loves historical research. What you do is go to the library and ask for the local history section, and sometimes you can ask for things they keep in store. Old papers. That sort of thing. And we must ask the vicar where the old church records are kept.' She put her arm through his, and turned him so that they could walk towards the church. 'Oh, do stick to it, Dan. It'll be a way of making you feel you belong here.'

'I feel that already,' Daniel said happily, knowing it was true.

When they reached the church porch, where the sunlight met peaceful shadows, Daniel stopped suddenly and faced his mother. 'Oh, and Mum, I want to ask you something. Something really important.'

'Yes, love?'

'What are we going to do about the old stove?'

'Mmmm, I don't know. But I must decide today. After you'd gone to bed last night we talked about it, and Dad said he was in favour of cleaning it up, re-blacking it, tiling behind it. Keeping it there, in other words.'

'Couldn't you display all your best pots on top?' asked Daniel hopefully.

'I suppose so,' she replied doubtfully, 'but I'd still rather rip it out. It's a bit of a monstrosity, Dan. Well, what do you think?'

'Why don't you let me make the final decision? The casting vote, and all that? It would be fair,' said Daniel.

Mrs Richards laughed. 'Oh you – you're just as bad as your father! All right then, what is it to be?'

Daniel put his hand on her arm, and spoke in his most

grown-up, determined voice, so that she looked slightly surprised.

'Mum,' he said, 'I want you to keep it there. I promise I'll clean it up myself, and make it look really nice – like something in a museum. But I really want to keep it – just to remind us of how things were. Just so's we don't forget.'

WOOF!   *Allan Ahlberg*

Eric is a perfectly ordinary boy. Perfectly ordinary that is, until the night when, safely tucked up in bed, he slowly but surely turns into a dog! Fritz Wagner's drawings illustrate this funny and exciting story superbly.

VERA PRATT AND THE FALSE MOUSTACHES   *Brough Girling*

There were times when Wally Pratt wished his mum was more ordinary and not the fanatic mechanic she was, but when he and his friends find themselves caught up in a real 'cops and robbers' affair, he is more than glad to have his mum, Vera, to help them.

SADDLEBOTTOM   *Dick King-Smith*

Hilarious adventures of a Wessex Saddleback pig whose white saddle is in the wrong place, to the chagrin of his mother.

SLADE   *John Tully*

Slade has a mission – to investigate life on Earth. When Eddie discovers the truth about Slade he gets a whole lot more adventure than he bargained for.

A TASTE OF BLACKBERRIES
Doris Buchanan Smith

The moving story about a young boy who has to come to terms with the tragic death of his best friend and the guilty feeling that he could somehow have saved him.

JELLYBEAN   *Tessa Duder*

A sensitive modern novel about Geraldine, alias 'Jellybean', who leads a rather solitary life as the only child of a single parent. She's tired of having to fit in with her mother's busy schedule, but a new friend and a performance of 'The Nutcracker Suite' change everything.

THE PRIESTS OF FERRIS   *Maurice Gee*

Susan Ferris and her cousin Nick return to the world of O which they had saved from the evil Halfmen, only to find that O is now ruled by cruel and ruthless priests. Can they save the inhabitants of O from tyranny? An action-packed and gripping story by the author of prize-winning THE HALF-MEN OF O.

THE SEA IS SINGING   *Rosalind Kerven*

In her seaside Shetland home, Tess is torn between the plight of the whales and loyalty to her father and his job on the oil rig. A haunting and thought-provoking novel.

BACK HOME   *Michelle Magorian*

A marvellously gripping story of an irrepressible girl's struggle to adjust to a new life. Twelve-year-old Rusty, who had been evacuated to the United States when she was seven, returns to the grey austerity of post-war Britain.

THE BEAST MASTER   *Andre Norton*

Spine-chilling science fiction – treachery and revenge! Hosteen Storm is a man with a mission to find and punish Brad Quade, the man who killed his father long ago on Terra, the planet where life no longer exists.

THE PRIME MINISTER'S BRAIN   *Gillian Cross*

The fiendish Demon Headmaster plans to gain control of No. 10 Downing Street and lure the Prime Minister into his evil clutches.

JASON BODGER AND
THE PRIORY GHOST   *Gene Kemp*

A ghost story, both funny and exciting, about Jason, the bane of every teacher's life, who is pursued by the ghost of a little nun from the twelfth century!

HALFWAY ACROSS THE GALAXY AND
TURN LEFT   *Robin Klein*

A humorous account of what happens to a family banished from their planet Zygron, when they have to spend a period of exile on Earth.

SUPERGRAN TO THE RESCUE   *Forrest Wilson*

The punchpacking, baddiebiffing escapades of the world's No. 1 senior citizen superhero – Super Gran! Now a devastating series on ITV!

TOM TIDDLER'S GROUND   *John Rowe Townsend*

Vic and Brain are given an old rowing boat which leads to the unravelling of a mystery and a happy reunion of two friends. An exciting adventure story.

THE FINDING *Nina Bawden*

Alex doesn't know his birthday because he was found abandoned next to Cleopatra's Needle, so instead of a birthday he celebrates his Finding. After inheriting an unexpected fortune, Alex's life suddenly becomes very exciting indeed.

RACSO AND THE RATS OF NIMH
Jane Leslie Conly

When fieldmouse Timothy Frisby rescues young Racso, the city rat, from drowning it's the beginning of a friendship and an adventure. The two are caught up in the struggle of the Rats of NIMH to save their home from destruction. A powerful sequel to MRS FRISBY AND THE RATS OF NIMH.

NICOBOBINUS *Terry Jones*

Nicobobinus and his friend, Rosie, find themselves in all sorts of intriguing adventures when they set out to find the Land of the Dragons long ago. Stunningly illustrated by Michael Foreman.

FRYING AS USUAL *Joan Lingard*

When Mr Francetti breaks his leg it looks as if his fish restaurant will have to close so Toni, Rosita and Paula decide to keep things going.

DRIFT *William Mayne*

A thrilling adventure of a young boy and an Indian girl, stranded on a frozen floating island in the North American wilderness.

Lights flicked on and house-doors opened all down the street, to watch the carnival set up. Montag and Beatty stared, one with dry satisfaction, the other with disbelief, at the house before them, this main ring in which torches would be juggled and fire eaten.

'Well,' said Beatty, 'now you *did* it. Old Montag wanted to fly near the sun and now that he's burnt his damn wings, he wonders why. Didn't I hint enough when I sent the Hound around your place?'

Montag's face was entirely numb and featureless; he felt his head turn like a stone carving to the dark place next door, set in its bright borders of flowers.

Beatty snorted. 'Oh, no! You weren't fooled by that little idiot's routine, now, were you? Flowers, butterflies, leaves, sunsets, oh, hell! It's all in her file. I'll be damned. I've hit the bullseye. Look at the sick look on your face. A few grassblades and the quarters of the moon. What trash. What good did she ever *do* with all that?'

Montag sat on the cold fender of the Dragon, moving his head half an inch to the left, half an inch to the right, left, right, left right, left . . .

'She saw everything. She didn't do anything to anyone. She just let them alone.'

'Alone, hell! She chewed around you, didn't she? One of those damn do-gooders with their shocked, holier-than-thou silences, their one talent making others feel guilty. God damn, they rise like the midnight sun to sweat you in your bed!'

The front door opened; Mildred came down the steps, running, one suitcase held with a dream-like clenching rigidity in her fist, as a beetle-taxi hissed to the kerb.

'Mildred!'

She ran past with her body stiff, her face floured with powder, her mouth gone, without lipstick.

'Mildred, you *didn't* put in the alarm!'

She shoved the valise in the waiting beetle, climbed in, and sat mumbling, 'Poor family, poor family, oh everything gone, everything, everything gone now . . .'

Beatty grabbed Montag's shoulder as the beetle blasted away and hit seventy miles an hour, far down the street, gone.

There was a crash like the falling parts of a dream fashioned out of warped glass, mirrors, and crystal prisms. Montag drifted about as if still another incomprehensible storm had turned him, to see Stoneman and Black wielding axes, shattering window-panes to provide cross-ventilation.

The brush of a death's-head moth against a cold black screen. 'Montag, this is Faber. Do you hear me? What is happening?'

'This is happening to *me*,' said Montag.

'What a dreadful surprise,' said Beatty. 'For everyone nowadays knows, absolutely is *certain*, that nothing will ever happen to *me*. Others die, *I* go on. There are no consequences and no responsibilities. Except that there *are*. But let's not talk about them, eh? By the time the consequences catch up with you, it's too late, isn't it, Montag?'

'Montag, can you get away, run?' asked Faber.

Montag walked but did not feel his feet touch the cement and then the night grasses. Beatty flicked his

igniter nearby and the small orange flame drew his fascinated gaze.

'What is there about fire that's so lovely? No matter what age we are, what draws us to it?' Beatty blew out the flame and lit it again. 'It's perpetual motion; the thing man wanted to invent but never did. Or almost perpetual motion. If you let it go on, it'd burn our lifetimes out. What is fire? It's a mystery. Scientists give us gobbledegook about friction and molecules. But they don't really know. Its real beauty is that it destroys responsibility and consequences. A problem gets too burdensome, then into the furnace with it. Now, Montag, you're a burden. And fire will lift you off my shoulders, clean, quick, sure; nothing to rot later. Antibiotic, aesthetic, practical.'

Montag stood looking in now at this queer house, made strange by the hour of the night, by murmuring neighbour voices, by littered glass, and there on the floor, their covers torn off and spilled out like swan-feathers, the incredible books that looked so silly and really not worth bothering with, for these were nothing but black type and yellowed paper and ravelled binding.

Mildred, of course. She must have watched him hide the books in the garden and brought them back in. Mildred. Mildred.

'I want you to do this job all by your lonesome, Montag. Not with kerosene and a match, but piecework, with a flame-thrower. Your house, your clean-up.'

'Montag, can't you run, get away!'

'No!' cried Montag helplessly. 'The Hound! Because of the Hound!'

Faber heard, and Beatty, thinking it was meant for him, heard. 'Yes, the Hound's somewhere about the neighbourhood, so don't try anything. Ready?'

123

'Ready.' Montag snapped the safety-catch on the flame-thrower.

'Fire!'

A great nuzzling gout of flame leapt out to lap at the books and knock them against the wall. He stepped into the bedroom and fired twice and the twin beds went up in a great simmering whisper, with more heat and passion and light than he would have supposed them to contain. He burnt the bedroom walls and the cosmetics chest because he wanted to change everything, the chairs, the tables, and in the dining-room the silverware and plastic dishes, everything that showed that he had lived here in this empty house with a strange woman who would forget him tomorrow, who had gone and quite forgotten him already, listening to her Seashell radio pour in on her and in on her as she rode across town, alone. And as before, it was good to burn, he felt himself gush out in the fire, snatch, rend, rip in half with flame, and put away the senseless problem. If there was no solution, well then now there was no problem, either. Fire was best for everything!

'The books, Montag!'

The books leapt and danced like roasted birds, their wings ablaze with red and yellow feathers.

And then he came to the parlour where the great idiot monsters lay asleep with their white thoughts and their snowy dreams. And he shot a bolt at each of the three blank walls and the vacuum hissed out at him. The emptiness made an even emptier whistle, a senseless scream. He tried to think about the vacuum upon which the nothingness had performed, but he could not. He held his breath so the vacuum could not get into his lungs. He cut off its terrible emptiness, drew back, and gave the entire room a gift of one huge bright yellow flower of

burning. The fire-proof plastic sheath on everything was cut wide and the house began to shudder with flame.

'When you're quite finished,' said Beatty behind him. 'You're under arrest.'

The house fell in red coals and black ash. It bedded itself down in sleepy pink-grey cinders and a smoke plume blew over it, rising and waving slowly back and forth in the sky. It was three-thirty in the morning. The crowd drew back into the houses; the great tents of the circus had slumped into charcoal and rubble and the show was well over.

Montag stood with the flame-thrower in his limp hands, great islands of perspiration drenching his armpits, his face smeared with soot. The other firemen waited behind him, in the darkness, their faces illuminated faintly by the smouldering foundation.

Montag started to speak twice and then finally managed to put his thought together.

'Was it my wife turned in the alarm?'

Beatty nodded. 'But her friends turned in an alarm earlier, that I let ride. One way or the other, you'd have got it. It was pretty silly, quoting poetry around free and easy like that. It was the act of a silly damn snob. Give a man a few lines of verse and he thinks he's the Lord of all Creation. You think you can walk on water with your books. Well, the world can get by just fine without them. Look where they got you, in slime up to your lip. If I stir the slime with my little finger, you'll drown!'

Montag could not move. A great earthquake had come with fire and levelled the house and Mildred was under there somewhere and his entire life under there and he could not move. The earthquake was still shaking and falling and shivering inside him and he stood there, his knees half-bent under the great load of tiredness and

bewilderment and outrage, letting Beatty hit him without raising a hand.

'Montag, you idiot, Montag, you damned fool; why did you *really* do it?'

Montag did not hear, he was far away, he was running with his mind, he was gone, leaving this dead soot-covered body to sway in front of another raving fool.

'Montag, get out of there!' said Faber.

Montag listened.

Beatty struck him a blow on the head that sent him reeling back. The green bullet in which Faber's voice whispered and cried, fell to the sidewalk. Beatty snatched it up, grinning. He held it half in, half out of his ear.

Montag heard the distant voice calling, 'Montag, you all right?'

Beatty switched the green bullet off and thrust it in his pocket. 'Well – so there's more here than I thought. I saw you tilt your head, listening. First I thought you had a Seashell. But when you turned clever later, I wondered. We'll trace this and drop it on your friend.'

'No!' said Montag.

He twitched the safety catch on the flame-thrower. Beatty glanced instantly at Montag's fingers and his eyes widened the faintest bit. Montag saw the surprise there and himself glanced to his hands to see what new thing they had done. Thinking back later he could never decide whether the hands or Beatty's reaction to the hands gave him the final push toward murder. The last rolling thunder of the avalanche stoned down about his ears, not touching him.

Beatty grinned his most charming grin. 'Well, that's one way to get an audience. Hold a gun on a man and force him to listen to your speech. Speech away. What'll it be this time? Why don't you belch Shakespeare at me,

you fumbling snob? "There is no terror, Cassius, in your threats, for I am arm'd so strong in honesty that they pass by me as an idle wind, which I respect not!" How's that? Go ahead now, you second-hand litterateur, pull the trigger.' He took one step toward Montag.

Montag only said, 'We never burned *right* . . .'

'Hand it over, Guy,' said Beatty with a fixed smile.

And then he was a shrieking blaze, a jumping, sprawling, gibbering mannikin, no longer human or known, all writhing flame on the lawn as Montag shot one continuous pulse of liquid fire on him. There was a hiss like a great mouthful of spittle banging a redhot stove, a bubbling and frothing as if salt had been poured over a monstrous black snail to cause a terrible liquefaction and a boiling over of yellow foam. Montag shut his eyes, shouted, shouted and fought to get his hands at his ears to clamp and to cut away the sound. Beatty flopped over and over and over, and at last twisted in on himself like a charred wax doll and lay silent.

The other two firemen did not move.

Montag kept his sickness down long enough to aim the flame-thrower. 'Turn around!'

They turned, their faces like blanched meat, streaming sweat; he beat their heads, knocking off their helmets and bringing them down on themselves. They fell and lay without moving.

The blowing of a single autumn leaf.

He turned and the Mechanical Hound was there.

It was half across the lawn, coming from the shadows, moving with such drifting ease that it was like a single solid cloud of black-grey smoke blown at him in silence.

It made a single last leap into the air, coming down at Montag from a good three feet over his head, its spidered legs reaching, the procaine needle snapping out its single

angry tooth. Montag caught it with a bloom of fire, a single wondrous blossom that curled in petals of yellow and blue and orange about the metal dog, clad it in a new covering as it slammed into Montag and threw him ten feet back against the bole of a tree, taking the flame-gun with him. He felt it scrabble and seize his leg and stab the needle in for a moment before the fire snapped the Hound up in the air, burst its metal bones at the joints, and blew out its interior in the single flushing of red colour like a skyrocket fastened to the street. Montag lay watching the dead-alive thing fiddle in the air and die. Even now it seemed to want to get back at him and finish the injection which was now working through the flesh of his leg. He felt all of the mingled relief and horror at having pulled back only in time to have just his knee slammed by the fender get up, afraid he might not be able to gain his feet at all, with an anaesthetized leg. A numbness in a numbness hollowed into a numbness . . .

And now . . .?

The street empty, the house burnt like an ancient bit of stage-scenery, the other homes dark, the Hound here, Beatty there, the two other firemen another place, and the Salamander . . .? He gazed at the immense engine. That would have to go, too.

Well, he thought, let's see how badly off you are. On your feet now. Easy, easy . . . *there*.

He stood and he had only one leg. The other was like a chunk of burnt pine-log he was carrying along as a penance for some obscure sin. When he put his weight on it, a shower of silver needles gushed up the length of the calf and went off in the knee. He wept. Come on! Come on, you, you can't stay here!

A few house-lights were going on again down the street, whether from the incidents just passed, or because of the

abnormal silence following the fight, Montag did not know. He hobbled around the ruins, seizing at his bad leg when it lagged, talking and whimpering and shouting directions at it and cursing it and pleading with it to work for him now when it was vital. He heard a number of people crying out in the darkness and shouting. He reached the back yard and the alley. Beatty, he thought, you're not a problem now. You always said, don't face a problem, burn it. Well, now I've done both. Good-bye, Captain.

And he stumbled along the alley in the dark.

A shotgun blast went off in his leg every time he put it down and he thought, you're a fool, a damn fool, an awful fool, an idiot, an awful idiot, a damn idiot, and a fool, a damn fool; look at the mess and where's the mop, look at the mess, and what do you do? Pride, damn it, and temper, and you've junked it all, at the very start you vomit on everyone and on yourself. But everything at once, but everything one on top of another, Beatty, the women, Mildred, Clarisse, everything. No excuse, though, no excuse. A fool, a damn fool, go give yourself up!

No, we'll save what we can, we'll do what there is left to do. If we have to burn, let's take a few more with us. Here!

He remembered the books and turned back. Just on the off chance.

He found a few books where he had left them, near the garden fence. Mildred, God bless her, had missed a few. Four books still lay hidden where he had put them. Voices were wailing in the night and flashbeams swirled about. Other Salamanders were roaring their engines far away,

and police cars were cutting their way across town with their sirens.

Montag took the four remaining books and hopped, jolted, hopped his way down the alley and suddenly fell as if his head had been cut off and only his body lay there. Something inside had jerked him to a halt and flopped him down. He lay where he had fallen and sobbed, his legs folded, his face pressed blindly to the gravel.

Beatty wanted to die.

In the middle of the crying Montag knew it for the truth. Beatty had wanted to die. He had just stood there, not really trying to save himself, just stood there, joking, needling, thought Montag, and the thought was enough to stifle his sobbing and let him pause for air. How strange, strange, to want to die so much that you let a man walk around armed and then instead of shutting up and staying alive, you go on yelling at people and making fun of them until you get them mad, and then . . .

At a distance, running feet.

Montag sat up. Let's get out of here. Come on, get up, get up, you just can't sit! But he was still crying and that had to be finished. It was going away now. He hadn't wanted to kill anyone, not even Beatty. His flesh gripped him and shrank as if it had been plunged in acid. He gagged. He saw Beatty, a torch, not moving, fluttering out on the grass. He bit at his knuckles. I'm sorry, I'm sorry, oh God, sorry . . .

He tried to piece it all together, to go back to the normal pattern of life a few short days ago before the sieve and the sand, Denham's Dentifrice, moth-voices, fireflies, the alarms and excursions, too much for a few short days, too much, indeed, for a lifetime.

Feet ran in the far end of the alley.

'Get up!' he told himself. 'Damn it, get up!' he said to

130

the leg, and stood. The pains were spikes driven in the kneecap and then only darning needles and then only common, ordinary safety pins, and after he had dragged along fifty more hops and jumps, filling his hand with slivers from the board fence, the prickling was like someone blowing a spray of scalding water on that leg. And the leg was at last his own leg again. He had been afraid that running might break the loose ankle. Now, sucking all the night into his open mouth, and blowing it out pale, with all the blackness left heavily inside himself, he set out in a steady jogging pace. He carried the books in his hands.

He thought of Faber.

Faber was back there in the steaming lump of tar that had no name or identity now. He had burnt Faber, too. He felt so suddenly shocked by this that he felt Faber was really dead, baked like a roach in that small green capsule shoved and lost in the pocket of a man who was now nothing but a frame skeleton strung with asphalt tendons.

You must remember, burn them or they'll burn you, he thought. Right now it's as simple as that.

He searched his pockets, the money was there, and in his other pocket he found the usual Seashell upon which the city was talking to itself in the cold black morning.

'Police Alert. Wanted: Fugitive in city. Has committed murder and crimes against the State. Name: Guy Montag. Occupation: Fireman. Last seen . . .'

He ran steadily for six blocks, in the alley, and then the alley opened out on to a wide empty thoroughfare ten lanes wide. It seemed like a boatless river frozen there in the raw light of the high white arc-lamps, you could drown trying to cross it, he felt; it was too wide, it was too open. It was a vast stage without scenery, inviting him to run

across, easily seen in the blazing illumination, easily caught, easily shot down.

The Seashell hummed in his ear.

'. . . watch for a man running . . . watch for the running man . . . watch for a man alone, on foot . . . watch . . .'

Montag pulled back into the shadows. Directly ahead lay a gas station, a great chunk of porcelain snow shining there, and two silver beetles pulling in to fill up. Now he must be clean and presentable if he wished to walk, not run, stroll calmly across that wide boulevard. It would give him an extra margin of safety if he washed up and combed his hair before he went on his way to get *where* . . .?

Yes, he thought, where *am* I running?

Nowhere. There was nowhere to go, no friend to turn to, really. Except Faber. And then he realized that he was indeed, running towards Faber's house, instinctively. But Faber couldn't hide him; it would be suicide even to try. But he knew that he would go to see Faber anyway, for a few short minutes. Faber's would be the place where he might refuel his vast draining belief in his own ability to survive. He just wanted to know that there was a man like Faber in the world. He wanted to see the man alive and not burned back there like a body shelled in another body. And some of the money must be left with Faber, of course, to be spent after Montag ran on his way. Perhaps he could make the open country and live on or near the rivers and near the highways, in the fields and hills.

A great whirling whisper made him look to the sky.

The police helicopters were rising so far away that it seemed someone had blown the grey head off a dry dandelion flower. Two dozen of them flurried, wavering, indecisive, three miles off, like butterflies puzzled by autumn, and then they were plummeting down to land, one by one, here, there, softly kneading the streets where,

turned back to beetles, they shrieked along the boulevards or, as suddenly, leapt back into the air, continuing their search.

And here was the gas station, its attendants busy now with customers. Approaching from the rear, Montag entered the men's washroom. Through the aluminium wall he heard a radio voice saying, 'War has been declared.' The gas was being pumped outside. The men in the beetles were talking and the attendants were talking about the engines, the gas, the money owed. Montag stood trying to make himself feel the shock of the quiet statement from the radio, but nothing would happen. The war would have to wait for him to come to it in his personal file, an hour, two hours from now.

He washed his hands and face and towelled himself dry, making little sound. He came out of the washroom and shut the door carefully and walked into the darkness and at last stood again on the edge of the empty boulevard.

There it lay, a game for him to win, a vast bowling alley in the cool morning. The boulevard was as clean as the surface of an arena two minutes before the appearance of certain un-named victims and certain unknown killers. The air over and above the vast concrete river trembled with the warmth of Montag's body alone; it was incredible how he felt his temperature could cause the whole immediate world to vibrate. He was a phosphorescent target; he knew it, he felt it. And now he must begin his little walk.

Three blocks away a few headlights glared. Montag drew a deep breath. His lungs were like burning brooms in his chest. His mouth was sucked dry from running. His

throat tasted of bloody iron and there was rusted steel in his feet.

What about those lights there? Once you started walking you'd have to gauge how fast those beetles could make it down here. Well, how far was it to the other kerb? It seemed like a hundred yards. Probably not a hundred, but figure for that anyway, figure that with him going very slowly, at a nice stroll, it might take as much as thirty seconds, forty seconds to walk all the way. The beetles? Once started, they could leave three blocks behind them in about fifteen seconds. So, even if halfway across he started to run . . .?

He put his right foot out and then his left foot and then his right. He walked on the empty avenue.

Even if the street were entirely empty, of course, you couldn't be sure of a safe crossing, for a car could appear suddenly over the rise four blocks further on and be on and past you before you had taken a dozen breaths.

He decided not to count his steps. He looked neither to left nor right. The light from the overhead lamps seemed as bright and revealing as the midday sun and just as hot.

He listened to the sound of the car picking up speed two blocks away on his right. Its movable headlights jerked back and forth suddenly, and caught at Montag.

Keep going.

Montag faltered, got a grip on the books, and forced himself not to freeze. Instinctively he took a few quick, running steps then talked out loud to himself and pulled up to stroll again. He was now half across the street, but the roar from the beetle's engines whined higher as it put on speed.

The police, of course. They see me. But slow now, slow, quiet, don't turn, don't look, don't seem concerned. Walk, that's it, walk, walk.

The beetle was rushing. The beetle was roaring. The beetle raised its speed. The beetle was whining. The beetle was in high thunder. The beetle came skimming. The beetle came in a single whistling trajectory, fired from an invisible rifle. It was up to 120 mph. It was up to 130 at least. Montag clamped his jaws. The heat of the racing headlights burnt his cheeks, it seemed, and jittered his eyelids and flushed the sour sweat out all over his body.

He began to shuffle idiotically and talk to himself and then he broke and just ran. He put out his legs as far as they would go and down and then far out again and down and back and out and down and back. God! God! He dropped a book, broke pace, almost turned, changed his mind, plunged on, yelling in concrete emptiness, the beetle scuttling after its running food, two hundred, one hundred feet away, ninety, eighty, seventy, Montag gasping, flailing his hands, legs up down out, up down out, closer, closer, hooting, calling, his eyes burnt white now as his head jerked about to confront the flashing glare, now the beetle was swallowed in its own light, now it was nothing but a torch hurtling upon him; all sound, all blare. Now – almost on top of him!

He stumbled and fell.

I'm done! It's over!

But the falling made a difference. An instant before reaching him the wild beetle cut and swerved out. It was gone. Montag lay flat, his head down. Wisps of laughter trailed back to him with the blue exhaust from the beetle.

His right hand was extended above him, flat. Across the extreme tip of his middle finger, he saw now as he lifted that hand, a faint sixteenth of an inch of black tread where tyre had touched in passing. He looked at that black line with disbelief, getting to his feet.

That wasn't the police, he thought.

He looked down the boulevard. It was clear now. A carful of children, all ages, God knew, from twelve to sixteen, out whistling, yelling, hurrahing, had seen a man, a very extraordinary sight, a man strolling, a rarity, and simply said, 'Let's get him,' not knowing he was the fugitive Mr Montag, simply a number of children out for a long night of roaring five or six hundred miles in a few moonlit hours, their faces icy with wind, and coming home or not coming at dawn, alive or not alive, that made the adventure.

They would have killed me, thought Montag, swaying, the air still torn and stirring about him in dust, touching his bruised cheek. For no reason at all in the world they would have killed me.

He walked toward the far kerb telling each foot to go and keep going. Somehow he had picked up the spilled books; he didn't remember bending or touching them. He kept moving them from hand to hand as if they were a poker hand he could not figure.

I wonder if they were the ones who killed Clarisse?

He stopped and his mind said it again, very loud.

I wonder if they were the ones who killed Clarisse!

He wanted to run after them yelling.

His eyes watered.

The thing that had saved him was falling flat. The driver of that car, seeing Montag down, instinctively considered the probability that running over a body at that speed might turn the car upside down and spill them out. If Montag had remained an upright target . . .?

Montag gasped.

Far down the boulevard, four blocks away, the beetle had slowed, spun about on two wheels, and was now racing back, slanting over on the wrong side of the street, picking up speed.

But Montag was gone, hidden in the safety of the dark alley for which he had set out on a long journey, an hour or was it a minute ago? He stood shivering in the night, looking back out as the beetle ran by and skidded back to the centre of the avenue, whirling laughter in the air all about it, gone.

Further on, as Montag moved in the darkness, he could see the helicopters falling, falling, like the first flakes of snow in the long winter to come . . .

The house was silent.

Montag approached from the rear, creeping through a thick night-moistened scent of daffodils and roses and wet grass. He touched the screen door in back, found it open, slipped in, moved across the porch, listening.

Mrs Black, are you asleep in there? he thought. This isn't good, but your husband did it to others and never asked and never wondered and never worried. And now since you're a fireman's wife, it's your home and your turn, for all the houses your husband burned and the people he hurt without thinking.

The house didn't reply.

He hid the books in the kitchen and moved from the house again to the alley and looked back and the house was still dark and quiet, sleeping.

On his way across town, with the helicopters fluttering like torn bits of paper in the sky, he phoned the alarm at a lonely phone booth outside a store that was closed for the night. Then he stood in the cold night air, waiting and at a distance he heard the fire sirens start up and run, and the Salamanders coming, coming to burn Mr Black's house while he was away at work, to make his wife stand shivering in the morning air while the roof let

go and dropped in upon the fire. But now, she was still asleep.

Good night, Mrs Black, he thought.

'Faber!'

Another rap, a whisper, and a long waiting. Then, after a minute, a small light flickered inside Faber's small house. After another pause, the back door opened.

They stood looking at each other in the half-light. Faber and Montag, as if each did not believe in the other's existence. Then Faber moved and put out his hand and grabbed Montag and moved him in and sat him down and went back and stood in the door, listening. The sirens were wailing off in the morning distance. He came in and shut the door.

Montag said, 'I've been a fool all down the line. I can't stay long. I'm on my way God knows where.'

'At least you were a fool about the right things,' said Faber. 'I thought you were dead. The audio-capsule I gave you – '

'Burnt.'

'I heard the captain talking to you and suddenly there was nothing. I almost came out looking for you.'

'The captain's dead. He found the audio-capsule, he heard your voice, he was going to trace it. I killed him with the flame-thrower.'

Faber sat down and did not speak for a time.

'My God, how did this happen?' said Montag. 'It was only the other night everything was fine and the next thing I know I'm drowning. How many times can a man go down and still be alive? I can't breathe. There's Beatty dead, and he was my friend once, and there's Millie gone, I thought she was my wife, but now I don't know. And the house all burnt. And my job gone and myself on the

run, and I planted a book in a fireman's house on the way. Good Christ, the things I've done in a single week!'

'You did what you had to do. It was coming on for a long time.'

'Yes, I believe that, if there's nothing else I believe. It saved itself up to happen. I could feel it for a long time, I was saving something up, I went around doing one thing and feeling another. God, it was all there. It's a wonder it didn't show on me, like fat. And now here I am, messing up your life. They might follow me here.'

'I feel alive for the first time in years,' said Faber. 'I feel I'm doing what I should have done a lifetime ago. For a little while I'm not afraid. Maybe it's because I'm doing the right thing at last. Maybe it's because I've done a rash thing and don't want to look the coward to you. I suppose I'll have to do even more violent things, exposing myself so I won't fall down on the job and turn scared again. What are your plans?'

'To keep running.'

'You know the war's on?'

'I heard.'

'God, isn't it funny?' said the old man. 'It seems so remote because we have our own troubles.'

'I haven't had time to think.' Montag drew out a hundred dollars. 'I want this to stay with you, use it any way that'll help when I'm gone.'

'But – '

'I might be dead by noon; use this.'

Faber nodded. 'You'd better head for the river if you can, follow it along, and if you can hit the old railroad lines going out into the country, follow them. Even though practically everything's airborne these days and most of the tracks are abandoned, the rails are still there, rusting. I've heard there are still hobo camps all across

139

the country, here and there; walking camps they call them, and if you keep walking far enough and keep an eye peeled, they say there's lots of old Harvard degrees on the tracks between here and Los Angeles. Most of them are wanted and hunted in the cities. They survive, I guess. There aren't many of them, and I guess the Government's never considered them a great enough danger to go in and track them down. You might hole up with them for a time and get in touch with me in St Louis. I'm leaving on the five A.M. bus this morning, to see a retired printer there, I'm getting out into the open myself, at last. The money will be put to good use. Thanks and God bless you. Do you want to sleep a few minutes?'

'I'd better run.'

'Let's check.'

He took Montag quickly into the bedroom and lifted a picture frame aside, revealing a television screen the size of a postal card. 'I always wanted something very small, something I could talk to, something I could blot out with the palm of my hand, if necessary, nothing that could shout me down, nothing monstrous big. So, you see.' He snapped it on.

'Montag,' the TV set said, and lit up. 'M-O-N-T-A-G.' The name was spelled out by the voice. 'Guy Montag. Still running. Police helicopters are up. A new Mechanical Hound has been brought from another district . . .'

Montag and Faber looked at each other.

'. . . Mechanical Hound *never* fails. Never since its first use in tracking quarry has this incredible invention made a mistake. Tonight, this network is proud to have the opportunity to follow the Hound by camera helicopter as it starts on its way to the target . . .'

Faber poured two glasses of whisky. 'We'll need these.'

They drank.

'. . . nose so sensitive the Mechanical Hound can remember and identify ten thousand odour-indexes on ten thousand men without re-setting!'

Faber trembled the least bit and looked about at his house, at the walls, the door, the doorknob, and the chair where Montag now sat. Montag saw the look. They both looked quickly about the house and Montag felt his nostrils dilate and he knew that he was trying to track himself and his nose was suddenly good enough to sense the path he had made in the air of the room and the sweat of his hand hung from the doorknob, invisible, but as numerous as the jewels of a small chandelier, he was everywhere, in and on and about everything, he was a luminous cloud, a ghost that made breathing once more impossible. He saw Faber stop up his own breath for fear of drawing that ghost into his own body, perhaps, being contaminated with the phantom exhalations and odours of a running man.

'The Mechanical Hound is now landing by helicopter at the site of the Burning!'

And there on the small screen was the burnt house, and the crowd, and something with a sheet over it and out of the sky, fluttering, came the helicopter like a grotesque flower.

So they must have their game out, thought Montag. The circus must go on, even with war beginning within the hour . . .

He watched the scene, fascinated, not wanting to move. It seemed so remote and no part of him; it was a play apart and separate, wondrous to watch, not without its strange pleasure. That's all for me, you thought, that's all taking place just for *me*, by God.

If he wished, he could linger here, in comfort, and follow the entire hunt on through its swift phases, down

alleys across streets, over empty running avenues, cross-ing lots and playgrounds, with pauses here or there for the necessary commercials, up other alleys to the burning house of Mr and Mrs Black, and so on finally to this house with Faber and himself seated, drinking, while the Electric Hound snuffed down the last trail, silent as a drift of death itself, skidded to a halt outside that window there. Then, if he wished, Montag might rise, walk to the window, keep one eye on the TV screen, open the window, lean out, look back, and see himself dramatized, described, made over, standing there, limned in the bright small television screen from outside, a drama to be watched objectively, knowing that in other parlours he was large as life, in full colour, dimensionally perfect! And if he kept his eye peeled quickly he would see himself, an instant before oblivion, being punctured for the benefit of how many civilian parlour-sitters who had been wakened from sleep a few minutes ago by the frantic sirening of their living-room walls to come watch the big game, the hunt, the one-man carnival.

Would he have time for a speech? As the Hound seized him, in view of ten or twenty or thirty million people, mightn't he sum up his entire life in the last week in one single phrase or a word that would stay with them long after the Hound had turned, clenching him in its metal-plier jaws, and trotted off in darkness, while the camera remained stationary, watching the creature dwindle in the distance – a splendid fade-out! What could he say in a single word, a few words, that would sear all their faces and wake them up?

'There,' whispered Faber.

Out of a helicopter glided something that was not machine, not animal, not dead, not alive, glowing with a pale green luminosity. It stood near the smoking ruins of

Montag's house and the men brought his discarded flame-thrower to it and put it down under the muzzle of the Hound. There was a whirring, clicking, humming.

Montag shook his head and got up and drank the rest of his drink. 'It's time. I'm sorry about this.'

'About what? Me? My house? I deserve everything. Run, for God's sake. Perhaps I can delay them here – '

'Wait. There's no use your being discovered. When I leave, burn the spread of this bed, that I touched. Burn the chair in the living room, in your wall incinerator. Wipe down the furniture with alcohol, wipe the door-knobs. Burn the throw-rug in the parlour. Turn the air-conditioning on full in all the rooms and spray with moth-spray if you have it. Then, turn on your lawn sprinklers as high as they'll go and hose off the sidewalks. With any luck at all, we can kill the trail *in* here, anyway.'

Faber shook his hand. 'I'll tend to it. Good luck. If we're both in good health, next week, the week after, get in touch. General Delivery, St Louis. I'm sorry there's no way I can go with you this time, by ear-phone. That was good for both of us. But my equipment was limited. You see, I never thought I would use it. What a silly old man. No thought there. Stupid, stupid. So I haven't another green bullet, the right kind, to put in your head. Go now!'

'One last thing. Quick. A suitcase, get it, fill it with your dirtiest clothes, an old suit, the dirtier the better, a shirt, some old sneakers and socks . . .'

Faber was gone and back in a minute. They sealed the cardboard valise with clear tape. 'To keep the ancient odour of Mr Faber in, of course,' said Faber sweating at the job.

Montag doused the exterior of the valise with whisky. 'I don't want that Hound picking up two odours at once.

143

May I take this whisky? I'll need it later. Christ I hope this works!'

They shook hands again and, going out of the door, they glanced at the TV. The Hound was on its way, followed by hovering helicopter cameras, silently, silently, sniffing the great night wind. It was running down the first alley.

'Good-bye!'

And Montag was out the back door lightly, running with the half-empty valise. Behind him he heard the lawn-sprinkling system jump up, filling the dark air with rain that fell gently and then with a steady pour all about, washing on the sidewalks, and draining into the alley. He carried a few drops of this rain with him on his face. He thought he heard the old man call good-bye, but he wasn't certain.

He ran very fast away from the house, down toward the river.

Montag ran.

He could feel the Hound, like autumn, come cold and dry and swift, like a wind that didn't stir grass, that didn't jar windows or disturb leaf-shadows on the white side-walks as it passed. The Hound did not touch the world. It carried its silence with it, so you could feel the silence building up a pressure behind you all across town. Montag felt the pressure rising, and ran.

He stopped for breath, on his way to the river, to peer through dimly lit windows of wakened houses, and saw the silhouettes of people inside watching their parlour walls and there on the walls the Mechanical Hound, a breath of neon vapour, spidered along, here and gone, here and gone! Now at Elm Terrace, Lincoln, Oak, Park, and up the alley toward Faber's house.

Go past, thought Montag, don't stop, go on, don't turn in!

On the parlour wall, Faber's house, with its sprinkler system pulsing in the night air.

The Hound paused, quivering.

No! Montag held to the window sill. This way! *Here!*

The procaine needle flicked out and in, out and in. A single clear drop of the stuff of dreams fell from the needle as it vanished in the Hound's muzzle.

Montag held his breath, like a doubled fist, in his chest.

The Mechanical Hound turned and plunged away from Faber's house down the alley again.

Montag snapped his gaze to the sky. The helicopters were closer, a great blowing of insects to a single light source.

With an effort, Montag reminded himself again that this was no fictional episode to be watched on his run to the river; it was in actuality his own chess-game he was witnessing, move by move.

He shouted to give himself the necessary push away from this last house window, and the fascinating seance going on in there! *Hell!* and he was away and gone! The alley, a street, the alley, a street, and the smell of the river. Leg out, leg down, leg out and down. Twenty million Montags running, soon, if the cameras caught him. Twenty million Montags running, running like an ancient flickery Keystone Comedy, cops, robbers, chasers and the chased, hunters and hunted, he had seen it a thousand times. Behind him now twenty million silently baying Hounds ricocheted across parlours, three-cushion shooting from right wall to centre wall to left wall, gone, right wall, centre wall, left wall, gone!

Montag jammed his Seashell to his ear.

'Police suggest entire population of the Elm Terrace

145

area do as follows: Everyone in every house in every street open a front or rear door or look from the windows. The fugitive cannot escape if everyone in the next minute looks from his house. Ready!'

Of course! Why hadn't they done it before! Why, in all the years, hadn't this game been tried! Everyone up, everyone out! He couldn't be missed! The only man running alone in the night city, the only man proving his legs!

'At the count of ten now! *One! Two!*'

He felt the city rise.

'Three!'

He felt the city turn to its thousands of doors.

Faster! Leg up, leg down!

'Four!'

The people sleepwalking in their hallways.

'Five!'

He felt their hands on the doorknobs!

The smell of the river was cool and like a solid rain. His throat was burnt rust and his eyes were wept dry with running. He yelled as if this yell would jet him on, fling him the last hundred yards.

'Six, seven, eight!'

The doorknobs turned on five thousand doors.

'Nine!'

He ran out away from the last row of houses, on a slope leading down to a solid moving blackness.

'Ten!'

The doors opened.

He imagined thousands on thousands of faces peering into yards, into alleys, and into the sky, faces hid by curtains, pale, night-frightened faces, like grey animals peering from electric caves, faces with grey colourless

146

eyes, grey tongues and grey thoughts looking out through the numb flesh of the face.

But he was at the river.

He touched it, just to be sure it was real. He waded in and stripped in darkness to the skin, splashed his body, arms, legs, and head with raw liquor; drank it and snuffed some up his nose. Then he dressed in Faber's old clothes and shoes. He tossed his own clothing into the river and watched it swept away. Then, holding the suitcase, he walked out in the river until there was no bottom and he was swept away in the dark.

He was three hundred yards downstream when the Hound reached the river. Overhead the great racketing fans of the helicopters hovered. A storm of light fell upon the river and Montag dived under the great illumination as if the sun had broken the clouds. He felt the river pull him further on its way, into darkness. Then the lights switched back to the land, the helicopters swerved over the city again, as if they had picked up another trail. They were gone. The Hound was gone. Now there was only the cold river and Montag floating in a sudden peacefulness, away from the city and the lights and the chase, away from everything.

He felt as if he had left a stage behind and many actors. He felt as if he had left the great seance and all the murmuring ghosts. He was moving from an unreality that was frightening into a reality that was unreal because it was new.

The black land slid by and he was going into the country among the hills. For the first time in a dozen years the stars were coming out above him, in great processions of wheeling fire. He saw a great juggernaut of stars form in the sky and threaten to roll over and crush him.

He floated on his back when the valise filled and sank; the river was mild and leisurely, going away from the people who ate shadows for breakfast and steam for lunch and vapours for supper. The river was very real; it held him comfortably and gave him the time at last, the leisure, to consider this month, this year, and a lifetime of years. He listened to his heart slow. His thoughts stopped rushing with his blood.

He saw the moon low in the sky now. The moon there, and the light of the moon caused by what? By the sun, of course. And what lights the sun? Its own fire. And the sun goes on, day after day, burning and burning. The sun and time. The sun and time and burning. Burning. The river bobbled him along gently. Burning. The sun and every clock on the earth. It all came together and became a single thing in his mind. After a long time of floating on the land and a short time of floating in the river he knew why he must never burn again in his life.

The sun burned every day. It burned Time. The world rushed in a circle and turned on its axis and time was busy burning the years and the people anyway, without any help from him. So if *he* burnt things with the firemen, and the sun burnt Time, that meant that *everything* burned!

One of them had to stop burning. The sun wouldn't, certainly. So it looked as if it had to be Montag and the people he had worked with until a few short hours ago. Somewhere the saving and the putting away had to begin again and someone had to do the saving and keeping, one way or another, in books, in records, in people's heads, any way at all so long as it was safe, free from moths, silver-fish, rust and dry-rot, and men with matches. The world was full of burning of all types and sizes. Now the guild of the asbestos-weaver must open shop very soon.

He felt his heel bump land, touch pebbles and rocks, scrape sand. The river had moved him toward shore.

He looked in at the great black creature without eyes or light, without shape, with only a size that went a thousand miles without wanting to stop, with its grass hills and forests that were waiting for him.

He hesitated to leave the comforting flow of the water. He expected the Hound there. Suddenly the trees might blow under a great wind of helicopters.

But there was only the normal autumn wind high up, going by like another river. Why wasn't the Hound running? Why had the search veered inland? Montag *listened*. Nothing. Nothing.

Millie, he thought. All this country here. Listen to it! Nothing and nothing. So much silence, Millie, I wonder how you'd take it? Would you shout Shut up, shut up! Millie, Millie. And he was sad.

Millie was not here and the Hound was not here, but the dry smell of hay blowing from some distant field put Montag on the land. He remembered a farm he had visited when he was very young, one of the rare times he had discovered that somewhere behind the seven veils of unreality, beyond the walls of parlours and beyond the tin moat of the city, cows chewed grass and pigs sat in warm ponds at noon and dogs barked after white sheep on a hill.

Now, the dry smell of hay, the motion of the waters, made him think of sleeping in fresh hay in a lonely barn away from the loud highways, behind a quiet farmhouse, and under an ancient windmill that whirred like the sound of the passing years overhead. He lay in the high barn loft all night, listening to distant animals and insects and trees, the little motions and stirrings.

During the night, he thought, below the loft, he would

hear a sound like feet moving, perhaps. He would tense and sit up. The sound would move away. He would lie back and look out of the loft window, very late in the night, and see the lights go out in the farmhouse itself, until a very young and beautiful woman would sit in an unlit window, braiding her hair. It would be hard to see her, but her face would be like the face of the girl so long ago in his past now, so very long ago, the girl who had known the weather and never been burned by the fireflies, the girl who had known what dandelions meant rubbed off on your chin. Then, she would be gone from the warm window and appear again upstairs in her moon-whitened room. And then, to the sound of death, the sound of the jets cutting the sky into two black pieces beyond the horizon, he would lie in the loft, hidden and safe, watching those strange new stars over the rim of the earth, fleeing from the soft colour of dawn.

In the morning he would not have needed sleep, for all the warm odours and sights of a complete country night would have rested and slept him while his eyes were wide and his mouth, when he thought to test it, was half a smile.

And there at the bottom of the hayloft stair, waiting for him, would be the incredible thing. He would step carefully down, in the pink light of early morning, so fully aware of the world that he would be afraid, and stand over the small miracle and at last bend to touch it.

A cool glass of fresh milk, and a few apples and pears laid at the foot of the steps.

This was all he wanted now. Some sign that the immense world would accept him and give him the long time needed to think all the things that must be thought.

A glass of milk, an apple, a pear.

He stepped from the river.

The land rushed at him, a tidal wave. He was crushed by darkness and the look of the country and the million odours on a wind that iced his body. He fell back under the breaking curve of darkness and sound and smell, his ears roaring. He whirled. The stars poured over his sight like flaming meteors. He wanted to plunge in the river again and let it idle him safely on down somewhere. This dark land rising was like that day in his childhood, swimming, when from nowhere the largest wave in the history of remembering slammed him down in salt and mud and green darkness, water burning mouth and nose, retching his stomach, screaming! Too much water!

Too much land!

Out of the black wall before him, a whisper. A shape. In the shape, two eyes. The night looking at him. The forest, seeing him.

The Hound!

After all the running and rushing and sweating it out and half-drowning, to come this far, work this hard, and think yourself safe and sigh with relief and come out on the land at last only to find . . .

The Hound!

Montag gave one last agonized shout as if this were too much for any man.

The shape exploded away. The eyes vanished. The leaf-piles flew up in a dry shower.

Montag was alone in the wilderness.

A deer. He smelled the heavy musk-like perfume mingled with blood and the gummed exhalation of the animal's breath, all cardamon and moss and ragweed odour in this huge night where the trees ran at him, pulled away, ran, pulled away, to the pulse of the heart behind his eyes.

There must have been a billion leaves on the land; he

waded in them, a dry river smelling of hot cloves and warm dust. And the other smells! There was a smell like a cut potato from all the land, raw and cold and white from having the moon on it most of the night. There was a smell like pickles from a bottle and a smell like parsley on the table at home. There was a faint yellow odour like mustard from a jar. There was a smell like carnations from the yard next door. He put down his hand and felt a weed rise up like a child brushing him. His fingers smelled of liquorice.

He stood breathing, and the more he breathed the land in, the more he was filled up with all the details of the land. He was not empty. There was more than enough here to fill him. There would always be more than enough.

He walked in the shallow tide of leaves, stumbling.

And in the middle of the strangeness, a familiarity.

His foot hit something that rang dully.

He moved his hand on the ground, a yard this way, a yard that.

The railroad track.

The track that came out of the city and rusted across the land, through forests and woods, deserted now, by the river.

Here was the path to wherever he was going. Here was the single familiar thing, the magic charm he might need a little while, to touch, to feel beneath his feet, as he moved on into the bramble bushes and the lakes of smelling and feeling and touching, among the whispers and the blowing down of leaves.

He walked on the track.

And he was surprised to learn how certain he suddenly was of a single fact he could not prove.

Once, long ago, Clarisse had walked here, where he was walking now.

*   *   *

152

Half an hour later, cold, and moving carefully on the tracks, fully aware of his entire body, his face, his mouth, his eyes stuffed with blackness, his ears stuffed with sound, his legs prickled with burrs and nettles, he saw the fire ahead.

The fire was gone, then back again, like a winking eye. He stopped, afraid he might blow the fire out with a single breath. But the fire was there and he approached warily, from a long way off. It took the better part of fifteen minutes before he drew very close indeed to it, and then he stood looking at it from cover. That small motion, the white and red colour, a strange fire because it meant a different thing to him.

It was not burning; it was *warming*!

He saw many hands held to its warmth, hands without arms, hidden in darkness. Above the hands, motionless faces that were only moved and tossed and flickered with firelight. He hadn't known fire could look this way. He had never thought in his life that it could give as well as take. Even its smell was different.

How long he stood he did not know, but there was a foolish and yet delicious sense of knowing himself as an animal come from the forest, drawn by the fire. He was a thing of brush and liquid eye, of fur and muzzle and hoof, he was a thing of horn and blood that would smell like autumn if you bled it out on the ground. He stood a long long time, listening to the warm crackle of the flames.

There was a silence gathered all about that fire and the silence was in the men's faces, and time was there, time enough to sit by this rusting track under the trees, and look at the world and turn it over with the eyes, as if it were held to the centre of the bonfire, a piece of steel these men were all shaping. It was not only the fire that was different. It was the silence. Montag moved toward

153

this special silence that was concerned with all of the world.

And then the voices began and they were talking, and he could hear nothing of what the voices said, but the sound rose and fell quietly and the voices were turning the world over and looking at it; the voices knew the land and the trees and the city which lay down the track by the river. The voices talked of everything, there was nothing they could not talk about, he knew from the very cadence and motion and continual stir of curiosity and wonder in them.

And then one of the men looked up and saw him, for the first or perhaps the seventh time, and a voice called to Montag:

'All right, you can come out now!'

Montag stepped back into the shadows.

'It's all right,' the voice said. 'You're welcome here.'

Montag walked slowly toward the fire and the five old men sitting there dressed in dark blue denim pants and jackets and dark blue suits. He did not know what to say to them.

'Sit down,' said the man who seemed to be the leader of the small group. 'Have some coffee?'

He watched the dark steaming mixture pour into a collapsible tin cup, which was handed him straight off. He sipped it gingerly and felt them looking at him with curiosity. His lips were scalded, but that was good. The faces around him were bearded, but the beards were clean, neat, and their hands were clean. They had stood up as if to welcome a guest, and now they sat down again. Montag sipped. 'Thanks,' he said. 'Thanks very much.'

'You're welcome, Montag. My name's Granger.' He held out a small bottle of colourless fluid. 'Drink this too. It'll change the chemical index of your perspiration. Half

an hour from now you'll smell like two other people. With the Hound after you, the best thing is Bottoms up.'

Montag drank the bitter fluid.

'You'll stink like a bobcat, but that's all right,' said Granger.

'You know my name,' said Montag.

Granger nodded to a portable TV set by the fire. 'We've watched the chase. Figured you'd wind up south along the river. When we heard you plunging around out in the forest like a drunken elk, we didn't hide as we usually do. We figured you were in the river, when the helicopter cameras swung back in over the city. Something funny there. The chase is still running. The other way, though.'

'The other way?'

'Let's have a look.'

Granger snapped the portable viewer on. The picture was a nightmare, condensed, easily passed from hand to hand, in the forest, all whirring colour and flight. A voice cried:

'The chase continues north in the city! Police helicopters are converging on Avenue 87 and Elm Grove Park!'

Granger nodded. 'They're faking. You threw them off at the river. They can't admit it. They know they can hold their audience only so long. The show's got to have a snap ending, quick! If they started searching the whole damn river it might take all night. So they're sniffing for a scapegoat to end things with a bang. Watch. They'll catch Montag in the next five minutes!'

'But how – '

'Watch.'

The camera, hovering in the belly of a helicopter, now swung down at an empty street.

'See that?' whispered Granger. 'It'll be you; right up at the end of that street is our victim. See how our camera is

coming in? Building the scene. Suspense. Long shot. Right now, some poor fellow is out for a walk. A rarity. An odd one. Don't think the police don't know the habits of queer ducks like that, men who walk mornings for the hell of it, or for reasons of insomnia. Anyway, the police have had him charted for months, years. Never know when that sort of information might be handy. And today, it turns out, it's very usable indeed. It saves face. Oh, God, look there!'

The men at the fire bent forward.

On the screen, a man turned a corner. The Mechanical Hound rushed forward into the viewer, suddenly. The helicopter light shot down a dozen brilliant pillars that built a cage all about the man.

A voice cried, 'There's Montag! The search is *done*!'

The innocent man stood bewildered, a cigarette burning in his hand. He stared at the Hound, not knowing what it was. He probably never knew. He glanced up at the sky and the wailing sirens. The cameras rushed down. The Hound leapt up into the air with a rhythm and a sense of timing that was incredibly beautiful. Its needle shot out. It was suspended for a moment in their gaze, as if to give the vast audience time to appreciate everything, the raw look of the victim's face, the empty street, the steel animal a bullet nosing the target.

'Montag, don't move!' said a voice from the sky.

The camera fell upon the victim, even as did the Hound. Both reached him simultaneously. The victim was seized by Hound and camera in a great spidering, clenching grip. He screamed. He screamed. He screamed!

Blackout.

Silence.

Darkness.

Montag cried out in the silence and turned away.

Silence.

And then, after a time of the men sitting around the fire, their faces expressionless, an announcer on the dark screen said, 'The search is over, Montag is dead; a crime against society has been avenged.'

Darkness.

'We now take you to the Sky Room of the Hotel Lux for a half-hour of Just-Before-Dawn, a programme of – '

Granger turned it off.

'They didn't show the man's face in focus. Did you notice? Even your best friends couldn't tell if it was you. They scrambled just enough to let the imagination take over. Hell,' he whispered. 'Hell.'

Montag said nothing but now, looking back, sat with his eyes fixed on the blank screen, trembling.

Granger touched Montag's arm. 'Welcome back from the dead.' Montag nodded. Granger went on. 'You might as well know all of us, now. This is Fred Clement, former occupant of the Thomas Hardy chair at Cambridge in the years before it became an Atomic Engineering School. The other is Dr Simmons from UCLA, a specialist in Ortega y Gasset; Professor West here did quite a bit for ethics, an ancient study now, for Columbia University quite some years ago. Reverend Padover here gave a few lectures thirty years ago and lost his flock between one Sunday and the next for his views. He's been bumming with us some time now. Myself: I wrote a book called *The Fingers in the Glove; the Proper Relationship between the Individual and Society*, and here I *am*! Welcome, Montag!'

'I don't belong with you,' said Montag, at last, slowly. 'I've been an idiot all the way.'

'We're used to that. We all made the *right* kind of mistakes, or we wouldn't be here. When we were separate

157

individuals, all we had was rage. I struck a fireman when he came to burn my library years ago. I've been running ever since. You want to join us, Montag?'

'Yes.'

'What have you to offer?'

'Nothing. I thought I had part of the Book of Ecclesiastes and maybe a little of Revelation, but I haven't even that now.'

'The Book of Ecclesiastes would be fine. Where was it?'

'Here,' Montag touched his head.

'Ah,' Granger smiled and nodded.

'What's wrong? Isn't that all right?' said Montag.

'Better than all right; perfect!' Granger turned to the Reverend. 'Do we have a Book of Ecclesiastes?'

'One. A man named Harris of Youngstown.'

'Montag.' Granger took Montag's shoulder firmly. 'Walk carefully. Guard your health. If anything should happen to Harris, *you* are the Book of Ecclesiastes. See how important you've become in the last minute!'

'But I've forgotten!'

'No, nothing's ever lost. We have ways to shake down your clinkers for you.'

'But I've tried to remember!'

'Don't try. It'll come when we need it. All of us have photographic memories, but spend a lifetime learning how to block off the things that are really *in* there. Simmons here has worked on it for twenty years and now we've got the method down to where we can recall anything that's been read once. Would you like, some day, Montag, to read Plato's *Republic*?'

'Of course!'

'*I* am Plato's *Republic*. Like to read Marcus Aurelius? Mr Simmons is Marcus.'

'How do you do?' said Mr Simmons.

'Hello,' said Montag.

'I want you to meet Jonathan Swift, the author of that evil political book, *Gulliver's Travels*! And this other fellow is Charles Darwin, and this one is Schopenhauer, and this one is Einstein, and this one here at my elbow is Mr Albert Schweitzer, a very kind philosopher indeed. Here we all are, Montag. Aristophanes and Mahatma Gandhi and Gautama Buddha and Confucius and Thomas Love Peacock and Thomas Jefferson and Mr Lincoln, if you please. We are also Matthew, Mark, Luke and John.'

Everyone laughed quietly.

'It can't *be*,' said Montag.

'It *is*,' replied Granger, smiling. '*We're* book-burners, too. We read the books and burnt them, afraid they'd be found. Micro-filming didn't pay off; we were always travelling, we didn't want to bury the film and come back later. Always the chance of discovery. Better to keep it in the old heads, where no one can see it or suspect it. We are all bits and pieces of history and literature and international law, Byron, Tom Paine, Machiavelli, or Christ, it's here. And the hour is late. And the war's begun. And we are out here, and the city is there, all wrapped up in its own coat of a thousand colours. What do you think, Montag?'

'I think I was blind trying to do things my way, planting books in firemen's houses and sending in alarms.'

'You did what you had to do. Carried out on a national scale, it might have worked beautifully. But our way is simpler and, we think, better. All we want to do is keep the knowledge we think we will need, intact and safe. We're not out to incite or anger anyone yet. For if we are destroyed, the knowledge is dead, perhaps for good. We are model citizens, in our own special way; we walk the

159

old tracks, we lie in the hills at night, and the city people let us be. We're stopped and searched occasionally, but there's nothing on our persons to incriminate us. The organization is flexible, very loose, and fragmentary. Some of us have had plastic surgery on our faces and fingerprints. Right now we have a horrible job; we're waiting for the war to begin and, as quickly, end. It's not pleasant, but then we're not in control, we're the odd minority crying in the wilderness. When the war's over, perhaps we can be of some use in the world.'

'Do you really think they'll listen then?'

'If not, we'll just have to wait. We'll pass the books on to our children, by word of mouth, and let our children wait, in turn, on the other people. A lot will be lost that way, of course. But you can't *make* people listen. They have to come round in their time, wondering what happened and why the world blew up under them. It can't last.'

'How many of you are there?'

'Thousands on the roads, the abandoned railtracks, tonight, bums on the outside, libraries inside. It wasn't planned, at first. Each man had a book he wanted to remember, and did. Then, over a period of twenty years or so, we met each other, travelling, and got the loose network together and set out a plan. The most important single thing we had to pound into ourselves was that we were not important, we mustn't be pedants; we were not to feel superior to anyone else in the world. We're nothing more than dust-jackets for books, of no significance otherwise. Some of us live in small towns. Chapter One of Thoreau's *Walden* in Green River, Chapter Two in Willow Farm, Maine. Why, there's one town in Maryland, only twenty-seven people, no bomb'll ever touch that town, is the complete essays of a man named Bertrand

160

Russell. Pick up that town, almost, and flip the pages, so many pages to a person. And when the war's over, some day, some year, the books can be written again, the people will be called in, one by one, to recite what they know and we'll set it up in type until another Dark Age, when we might have to do the whole damn thing over again. But that's the wonderful thing about man; he never gets so discouraged or disgusted that he gives up doing it all over again, because he knows very well it is important and *worth* the doing.'

'What do we do tonight?' asked Montag.

'Wait,' said Granger. 'And move downstream a little way, just in case.'

He began throwing dust and dirt on the fire.

The other men helped, and Montag helped, and there, in the wilderness, the men all moved their hands, putting out the fire together.

They stood by the river in the starlight.

Montag saw the luminous dial of his waterproof. Five. Five o'clock in the morning. Another year ticked by in a single hour, and dawn waiting beyond the far bank of the river.

'Why do you trust me?' said Montag.

A man moved in the darkness.

'The look of you's enough. You haven't seen yourself in a mirror lately. Beyond that, the city has never cared so much about us to bother with an elaborate chase like this to find us. A few crackpots with verses in their heads can't touch them, and they know it and we know it; everyone knows it. So long as the vast population doesn't wander about quoting the Magna Charta and the Constitution, it's all right. The firemen were enough to check that, now and then. No, the cities don't bother us. And *you* look like hell.'

161

They moved along the bank of the river, going south. Montag tried to see the men's faces, the old faces he remembered from the firelight, lined and tired. He was looking for a brightness, a resolve, a triumph over tomorrow that hardly seemed to be there. Perhaps he had expected their faces to burn and glitter with the knowledge they carried, to glow as lanterns glow, with the light in them. But all the light had come from the camp fire, and these men had seemed no different from any others who had run a long race, searched a long search, seen good things destroyed, and now, very late, were gathering to wait for the end of the party and the blowing out of the lamps. They weren't at all certain that the things they carried in their heads might make every future dawn glow with a purer light, they were sure of nothing save that the books were on file behind their quiet eyes, the books were waiting, with their pages uncut, for the customers who might come by in later years, some with clean and some with dirty fingers.

Montag squinted from one face to another as they walked.

'Don't judge a book by its cover,' someone said.

And they all laughed quietly, moving downstream.

There was a shriek and the jets from the city were gone overhead long before the men looked up. Montag stared back at the city, far down the river, only a faint glow now.

'My wife's back there.'

'I'm sorry to hear that. The cities won't do well in the next few days,' said Granger.

'It's strange, I don't miss her, it's strange I don't feel much of anything,' said Montag. 'Even if she dies, I realized a moment ago, I don't think I'll feel sad. It isn't right. Something must be wrong with me.'

162

'Listen,' said Granger, taking his arm, and walking with him, holding aside the bushes to let him pass. 'When I was a boy my grandfather died, and he was a sculptor. He was also a very kind man who had a lot of love to give the world, and he helped clean up the slum in our town; and he made toys for us and he did a million things in his lifetime; he was always busy with his hands. And when he died, I suddenly realized I wasn't crying for him at all, but for the things he did. I cried because he would never do them again, he would never carve another piece of wood or help us raise doves and pigeons in the back yard or play the violin the way he did, or tell us the jokes the way he did. He was part of us and when he died, all the actions stopped dead and there was no one to do them just the way he did. He was individual. He was an important man. I've never gotten over his death. Often I think, what wonderful carvings never came to birth because he died. How many jokes are missing from the world, and how many homing pigeons untouched by his hands. He shaped the world. He *did* things to the world. The world was bankrupted of ten million fine actions the night he passed on.'

Montag walked in silence. 'Millie, Millie,' he whispered. 'Millie.'

'What?'

'My wife, my wife. Poor Millie, poor Millie. I can't remember anything. I think of her hands but I don't see them doing anything at all. They just hang there at her sides or they lie there on her lap or there's a cigarette in them, but that's all.'

Montag turned and glanced back.

What did you give to the city, Montag?

Ashes.

What did the others give to each other?

163

Nothingness.

Granger stood looking back with Montag. 'Everyone must leave something behind when he dies, my grandfather said. A child or a book or a painting or a house or a wall built or a pair of shoes made. Or a garden planted. Something your hand touched some way so your soul has somewhere to go when you die, and when people look at that tree or that flower you planted, you're there. It doesn't matter what you do, he said, so long as you change something from the way it was before you touched it into something that's like you after you take your hands away. The difference between the man who just cuts lawns and a real gardener is in the touching, he said. The lawn-cutter might just as well not have been there at all; the gardener will be there a lifetime.'

Granger moved his hand. 'My grandfather showed me some V-2 rocket films once, fifty years ago. Have you ever seen the atom-bomb mushroom from two hundred miles up? It's a pinprick, it's nothing. With the wilderness all around it.

'My grandfather ran off the V-2 rocket film a dozen times and then hoped that some day our cities would open up and let the green and the land and the wilderness in more, to remind people that we're allotted a little space on earth and that we survive in that wilderness that can take back what it has given, as easily as blowing its breath on us or sending the sea to tell us we are not so big. When we forget how close the wilderness is in the night, my grandpa said, some day it will come in and get us, for we will have forgotten how terrible and real it can be. You see?' Granger turned to Montag. 'Grandfather's been dead for all these years, but if you lifted my skull, by God, in the convolutions of my brain you'd find the big ridges of his thumbprint. He touched me. As I said

164

earlier, he was a sculptor. "I hate a Roman named Status Quo!" he said to me. "Stuff your eyes with wonder," he said, "live as if you'd drop dead in ten seconds. See the world. It's more fantastic than any dream made or paid for in factories. Ask no guarantees, ask for no security, there never was such an animal. And if there were, it would be related to the great sloth which hangs upside down in a tree all day every day, sleeping its life away. To hell with that," he said, "shake the tree and knock the great sloth down on his ass." '

'Look!' cried Montag.

And the war began and ended in that instant.

Later, the men around Montag could not say if they had really seen anything. Perhaps the merest flourish of light and motion in the sky. Perhaps the bombs were there, and the jets, ten miles, five miles, one mile up, for the merest instant, like grain thrown over the heavens by a great sowing hand, and the bombs drifting with dreadful swiftness, yet sudden slowness, down upon the morning city they had left behind. The bombardment was to all intents and purposes finished, once the jets had sighted their target, alerted their bombardiers at five thousand miles an hour; as quick as the whisper of a scythe the war was finished. Once the bomb-release was yanked it was over. Now, a full three seconds, all of the time in history, before the bombs struck, the enemy ships themselves were gone half around the visible world, like bullets in which a savage islander might not believe because they were invisible; yet the heart is suddenly shattered, the body falls in separate motions and the blood is astonished to be freed on the air; the brain squanders its few precious memories and, puzzled, dies.

This was not to be believed. It was merely a gesture. Montag saw the flirt of a great metal fist over the far city

and he knew the scream of the jets that would follow, would say, after the deed, *disintegrate, leave no stone on another, perish. Die*.

Montag held the bombs in the sky for a single moment, with his mind and his hands reaching helplessly up at them. 'Run!' he cried to Faber. To Clarisse, 'Run!' To Mildred, 'Get out, get out of there!' But Clarisse, he remembered, was dead. And Faber *was* out; there in the deep valleys of the country somewhere the five A.M. bus was on its way from one desolation to another. Though the desolation had not yet arrived, was still in the air, it was certain as man could make it. Before the bus had run another fifty yards on the highway, its destination would be meaningless, and its point of departure changed from metropolis to junkyard.

And Mildred . . .

Get out, run!

He saw her in her hotel room somewhere now in the half-second remaining with the bombs a yard, a foot, an inch from her building. He saw her leaning toward the great shimmering walls of colour and motion where the family talked and talked and talked to her, where the family prattled and chatted and said her name and smiled at her and said nothing of the bomb that was an inch, now a half-inch, now a quarter-inch from the top of the hotel. Leaning into the wall as if all of the hunger of looking would find the secret of her sleepless unease there. Mildred, leaning anxiously, nervously, as if to plunge, drop, fall into that swarming immensity of colour to drown in its bright happiness.

The first bomb struck.

'Mildred!'

Perhaps, who would ever know? Perhaps the great

166

broadcasting stations with their beams of colour and light and talk and chatter went first into oblivion.

Montag, falling flat, going down, saw or felt, or imagined he saw or felt the walls go dark in Millie's face, heard her screaming, because in the millionth part of time left, she saw her own face reflected there, in a mirror instead of a crystal ball, and it was such a wildly empty face, all by itself in the room, touching nothing, starved and eating of itself, that at last she recognized it as her own and looked quickly up at the ceiling as it and the entire structure of the hotel blasted down upon her, carrying her with a million pounds of brick, metal, plaster, and wood, to meet other people in the hives below, all on their quick way down to the cellar where the explosion rid itself of them in its own unreasonable way.

I remember. Montag clung to the earth. I remember. Chicago. Chicago, a long time ago. Millie and I. *That's* where we met! I remember now. Chicago. A long time ago.

The concussion knocked the air across and down the river, turned the men over like dominoes in a line, blew the water in lifting sprays, and blew the dust and made the trees above them mourn with a great wind passing away south. Montag crushed himself down, squeezing himself small, eyes tight. He blinked once. And in that instant saw the city, instead of the bombs, in the air. They had displaced each other. For another of those impossible instants the city stood, rebuilt and unrecognizable, taller than it had ever hoped or strived to be, taller than man had built it, erected at last in gouts of shattered concrete and sparkles of torn metal into a mural hung like a reversed avalanche, a million colours, a million oddities, a door where a window should be, a top for a bottom, a

side for a back, and then the city rolled over and fell down dead.

The sound of its death came after.

Montag, lying there, eyes gritted shut with dust, a fine wet cement of dust in his now shut mouth, gasping and crying, now thought again, I remember, I remember, I remember something else. What is it? Yes, yes, part of the Ecclesiastes and Revelation. Part of that book, part of it, quick now, quick, before it gets away, before the shock wears off, before the wind dies. Book of Ecclesiastes. Here. He said it over to himself silently, lying flat to the trembling earth, he said the words of it many times and they were perfect without trying and there was no Denham's Dentifrice anywhere, it was just the Preacher by himself, standing there in his mind, looking at him . . .

'There,' said a voice.

The men lay gasping like fish laid out on the grass. They held to the earth as children hold to familiar things, no matter how cold or dead, no matter what has happened or will happen, their fingers were clawed into the dirt, and they were all shouting to keep their eardrums from bursting, to keep their sanity from bursting, mouths open, Montag shouting with them, a protest against the wind that ripped their faces and tore at their lips, making their noses bleed.

Montag watched the great dust settle and the great silence move down upon their world. And lying there it seemed that he saw every single grain of dust and every blade of grass and that he heard every cry and shout and whisper going up in the world now. Silence fell down in the sifting dust, and all the leisure they might need to look around, to gather the reality of this day into their senses.

Montag looked at the river. We'll go on the river. He looked at the old railroad tracks. Or we'll go that way. Or we'll walk on the highways now, and we'll have time to put things into ourselves. And some day, after it sets in us a long time, it'll come out of our hands and our mouths. And a lot of it will be wrong, but just enough of it will be right. We'll just start walking today and see the world and the way the world walks around and talks, the way it really looks. I want to see everything now. And while none of it will be me when it goes in, after a while it'll all gather together inside and it'll be me. Look at the world out there, my God, my God, look at it out there, outside me, out there beyond my face and the only way to really touch it is to put it where it's finally me, where it's in the blood, where it pumps around a thousand times ten thousand a day. I get hold of it so it'll never run off. I'll hold on to the world tight some day. I've got one finger on it now; that's a beginning.

The wind died.

The other men lay a while, on the dawn edge of sleep, not yet ready to rise up and begin the day's obligations, its fires and foods, its thousand details of putting foot after foot and hand after hand. They lay blinking their dusty eyelids. You could hear them breathing fast, then slower, then slow . . .

Montag sat up.

He did not move any further, however. The other men did likewise. The sun was touching the black horizon with a faint red tip. The air was cold and smelled of a coming rain.

Silently, Granger arose, felt his arms, and legs, swearing, swearing incessantly under his breath, tears dripping from his face. He shuffled down to the river to look upstream.

'It's flat,' he said, a long time later. 'City looks like a heap of baking-powder. It's gone.' And a long time after that. 'I wonder how many knew it was coming? I wonder how many were surprised?'

And across the world, thought Montag, how many other cities dead? And here in our country, how many? A hundred, a thousand?

Someone struck a match and touched it to a piece of dry paper taken from their pocket, and shoved this under a bit of grass and leaves, and after a while added tiny twigs which were wet and sputtered but finally caught, and the fire grew larger in the early morning as the sun came up and the men slowly turned from looking up river and were drawn to the fire, awkwardly, with nothing to say, and the sun coloured the backs of their necks as they bent down.

Granger unfolded an oilskin with some bacon in it. 'We'll have a bite. Then we'll turn around and walk upstream. They'll be needing us up that way.'

Someone produced a small frying-pan and the bacon went into it and the frying-pan was set on the fire. After a moment the bacon began to flutter and dance in the pan and the sputter of it filled the morning air with its aroma. The men watched this ritual silently.

Granger looked into the fire. 'Phoenix.'

'What?'

'There was a damn silly bird called a Phoenix back before Christ: every few hundred years he built a pyre and burned himself up. He must have been first cousin to Man. But every time he burnt himself up he sprang out of the ashes, he got himself born all over again. And it looks like we're doing the same thing, over and over, but we've got one damn thing the Phoenix never had. We know the damn silly thing we just did. We know all the damn silly

things we've done for a thousand years, and as long as we know that and always have it around where we can see it, some day we'll stop making the goddam funeral pyres and jumping into the middle of them. We pick up a few more people that remember, every generation.'

He took the pan off the fire and let the bacon cool and they ate it, slowly, thoughtfully.

'Now, let's get on upstream,' said Granger. 'And hold on to one thought: You're not important. You're not anything. Some day the load we're carrying with us may help someone. But even when we had the books on hand, a long time ago, we didn't use what we got out of them. We went right on insulting the dead. We went right on spitting in the graves of all the poor ones who died before us. We're going to meet a lot of lonely people in the next week and the next month and the next year. And when they ask us what we're doing, you can say, We're remembering. That's where we'll win out in the long run. And some day we'll remember so much that we'll build the biggest goddam steam-shovel in history and dig the biggest grave of all time and shove war in and cover it up. Come on now, we're going to go build a mirror-factory first and put out nothing but mirrors for the next year and take a long look in them.'

They finished eating and put out the fire. The day was brightening all about them as if a pink lamp had been given more wick. In the trees, the birds that had flown away now came back and settled down.

Montag began walking and after a moment found that the others had fallen in behind him, going north. He was surprised, and moved aside to let Granger pass, but Granger looked at him and nodded him on. Montag went ahead. He looked at the river and the sky and the rusting track going back down to where the farms lay, where the

171

barns stood full of hay, where a lot of people had walked by in the night on their way from the city. Later, in a month or six months, and certainly not more than a year, he would walk along here again, alone, and keep right on going until he caught up with the people.

But now there was a long morning's walk until noon, and if the men were silent it was because there was everything to think about and much to remember. Perhaps later in the morning, when the sun was up and had warmed them, they would begin to talk, or just say the things they remembered, to be sure they were there, to be absolutely certain that things were safe in them. Montag felt the slow stir of words, the slow simmer. And when it came to his turn, what could he say, what could he offer on a day like this, to make the trip a little easier? To everything there is a season. Yes. A time to break down, and a time to build up. Yes. A time to keep silence and a time to speak. Yes, all that. But what else. What else? Something, something . . .

And on either side of the river was there a tree of life,
which bare twelve manner of fruits, and yielded her fruit
every month; And the leaves of the tree were for the healing
of the nations.

Yes, thought Montag, that's the one I'll save for noon. For noon . . .

When we reach the city.